August 1

My God! I can't believe we finally made it. It's been close to four months and Lord knows it hasn't been easy. The people are all but worn out but just seeing Free Town has given them all hope. It is just a bunch of tents and lean to's right now but the men are already gathering materials for homes and with the beauty of the landscape with its rolling hills and valleys we should be able to eke out a relatively good existence. And aside from the one army incursion things here seem peaceful enough.

It is good seeing everyone together once again. It's almost as if it were a homecoming of sorts. Three Winds has always been a tight knit family. Still, with everyone here again my thoughts still go back to my father and my uncle the two most important men in my life. They have always been there for me for as long as I can remember. Now suddenly they're gone and I feel as if I have the weight of the world on my shoulders. Here in a foreign land I must lead in the building of a community we can all love and take pride in.

I can only thank God that mama and Aunt Petunia are still here to help give me guidance. I will also rely on my friend Crooked Nose to sketch the lay of the land and provide caution when needed.

I've chosen a prime piece of land to build our ranch on and I think Mandy is even more excited than I am about our new beginning. The land we picked has two rolling streams running through it and a pecan grove already in place. And there are acres and acres of plush grasslands on the prairie making it simply ideal to raise horses. Four foals were born over the four month trek. We have close to a hundred horses now and Uncle Andrew would be proud. With more and more settlers moving West fresh thoroughbred horses will prove invaluable.

Aunt Petunia has given me charge of my uncle's horses and I've already hired six of Crooked Nose's braves to help break and train them as they are quite good horsemen. That will be the first order of business since we will have to depend on their sale and trade for our sustenance.

I've also started on the construction of our home. As Aunt Petunia and the others arrived weeks before we did most of their homes are already under construction. Still, those soldiers that have little to do when they are not training and have some extra time on their hands and need the extra money to procure things in this new land are now in my employ. At this rate our new home should be completed within a month. Most of the

men are building their own homes and when not are chipping in to help a neighbor build theirs.

I must honestly say that I can't ever remember seeing morale so high. It's almost as if they have finally escaped from the cruelty that is racism. It's almost as if they have flung the shackles of slavery into the distant winds and are finally free.

I can see it in the children's faces as I watch them roll in the prairie grass laughing and giggling. I even see mama smiling and singing as she goes about her daily chores.

"Hello my friend."

"And what do we owe this visit?" I said eyeing my friend Crooked Nose wearily as I continued to work on the front porch. I'd come to know this man enough to know that there was something weighing heavily on his mind. Usually jovial and smiling there was no smile now as he rode up.

"What is it my friend?"

"I have grave news for you my friend."

"Then you must share it with me at once," I said never having been one to postpone the inevitable.

"It seems that the government is disbanding the troops at Fort Arbuckle and transferring them to Fort Sill."

I knew little of the politics of the plains or what Crooked Nose was getting at. Seeing my confusion he went on.

"Don't you see? They are sending the Buffalo Soldiers away to watch the border of Texas and Mexico. They say it is to stop the border raids by the Comanche and Apaches but that is not the reason."

I sat now and invited Crooked Nose to sit across from me but there was no pipe to share this time.

"They are sending the Buffalo Soldiers away. They are with the U.S. Calvary but they are not the same. In the six years they have been stationed at Fort Arbuckle we have never had a confrontation or encounter. They are like you. Some come and visit with me and eat with my family. We have become friends. Yes, they too are soldiers but they are not filled with the same hatred as the white soldiers sent here and because of that they are being sent away."

"That doesn't make sense. But what does that mean for us?"

"I have seen this before Caesar. What is happening is the U.S. government is going to come in and allow those heading for the California gold fields to cross our lands with impunity and unencumbered. Any sight of us will be looked at as hostile. Any resistance to the settlers and it will be thought of as an act of war and looked at as if we have broken the peace treaty giving them the rights to our lands. And that is what they

want. They are trying to provoke us into a war so they can steal more of our lands. I have seen it happen too many times before."

"So, what are we to do?"

"There is little any of us can do. We can stand like men and fight this takeover or we can act like old women and cry in our blankets."

"Those are the choices?"

"I am afraid so my friend."

"Then when that day comes know only that I will be by your side."

"And for that I am grateful Caesar. How is your mother?"

"That's a good question. She seems to be doing fine. But then if she wasn't I would hardly know."

Crooked Nose laughed.

"Yes. She is a strong woman. Where is she now?"

"I believe she is over by the North Fork."

"I think I would like to see how my friend is holding up. Don't tell her this but I miss our long talks."

Caesar smiled.

"Come. I will take you to see her now," Caesar said before grabbing his big, grey sorrel and mounting it.

"How is the corral coming?"

"Good."

Caesar had chosen a fairly large canyon with an entry only wide enough for a single horse to get through with tall plains grass and a wall of rock which would prove a natural shelter from the elements. Now after several days of clearing the brush and other fallen debris it made a plush pasture and surprisingly large enough to hold the whole herd.

"Mother are you home?" Caesar said knocking at the modest little three room home. Fiona and Petunia's homes had been the first to be built and with over a hundred laboring day and night it took only a few short weeks to have the homes constructed. The men proposed a house suitable for the matriarchs but Fiona had vehemently objected. She no longer needed a big house as she did following slavery but now only something

that represented her. And so she had a simple little, three room frame house built for herself and Jeremiah when he returned.

"Mother."

"I'm here Caesar. What's all the commotion?"

"You have a visitor mother."

Coming from the bedroom Fiona smiled when she saw Crooke Nose.

"Well, well, well. What a pleasant surprise. I see Light Feather let you out?"

"I am chief of the people. I am the greatest chief the Northern Cheyenne has ever known. No woman dictates what I do," Crooked Nose said once again exacerbated by this tiny woman. "I do not know why I came by here to check on you. You are nothing but a mean old woman who likes to anger me, an old man."

Fiona laughed.

"You came by to see me because you realize that after having met me life would not be the same if you were not to speak with me."

"You think a lot of yourself woman. But if when my braves return with news of your husband we will see. I hope you are praying to your great white god that he is alive.

If he is not I will take you as my fourth wife and assign you the duties of cooking and waiting on your chief as a woman should. And I will have that sharp tongue of yours sewn to the back of your head so you cannot speak such vile thoughts to the chief of the Northern Cheyenne."

Mama laughed heartily and I knew the two friends were glad to see each other once again.

"Sit down. I've just made some venison stew and biscuits. Sit! Sit! And tell me the news of Light Feather and my friend Stands with a Fist."

Soon the two were caught up in a lively conversation though I am not sure that either understood much of what the other was saying without Thomas to interpret. Still, after mama pulled out the hooch and they both sat down to a few rounds it hardly seemed to matter as they both drank too much and laughed heartily.

The news from Crooked Nose hadn't been good but it gave warning that life here on the plains was not to come without some heartache. I couldn't think about that now though. There was much to be done before the winter snows hit. Tomorrow I would go along with a small contingent of settlers and troops to Fort Arbuckle to meet with these Buffalo Soldiers Crooked Nose thought so highly of and purchase the much needed supplies and hopefully sell some horses.

August 2

"Caesar. Caesar. You told me to wake you at five."

I groaned and rolled over. Ever since we had arrived at Free Town I had been going. If it weren't helping some old woman unload her wagon then it was aiding one of my people in the construction of their home. I don't think I was doing anymore than the next man but it sure as hell felt like it. I was exhausted and was surely not looking forward to the two hour ride between Free Town and Fort Arbuckle.

"Mandy please tell me it's not five already?"

"I can't lie Caesar," Mandy said smiling at me before letting her sheer black nightgown slip from her ebony body and hit the floor. "But if I don't catch you when I can I may never get another chance she said climbing back in bed before straddling me and taking me in her. It had been awhile since I lain with the mother of my child and I could tell Mandy was in dire need the way she went about it. When she'd finally come for the third or fourth time Mandy screamed loud enough to wake up all of Free Town. When it was over and I knew she was spent and had had enough I got up dressed quickly and headed for the creek to wash up.

I was quite surprised to find anyone up at this hour but there was Monica down at the creek. I can't say for sure but I'd say Monica was about twenty, maybe twenty-one and one of the many who had flocked to Three Winds following the war looking for asylum. I'd seen her around and I have to admit she'd caught my eye on more than one occasion. Long and tall, she was more than a little attractive with her gray eyes and long, straight black hair. A mulatto or mixed blood we'd flirted on more than one occasion but something had always come up that prevented me from getting to know her better. She was certainly more than willing and I'd made a mental note to get to know her better but like I said something always came up.

Now that Mandy had staked her claim it seemed out of the question but here she was. Mandy hadn't helped any when she'd seemingly taken the girl under her wing and given her the job of helping her take care of the baby while she went about her daily chores and went back to school to learn to read and write hoping to be a better wife and help me out with the books.

When she proposed to have a cabin built right there on our property for the girl I protested but Mandy was insistent and I had more pressing matters to deal with than to argue with Mandy.

"How are you this morning Caesar?"

"Fair to middlin' and you?"

"I'm not sure. I gave thanks and praise this mo'nin' when I got up but then I heard these screams as I was headed down here to do the wash and I said Lord if you can grant me one small blessing please let Caesar bestow some of that good ol' time religion on me and let me sing your praises just like Miss Mandy be doing," the girl laughed.

I dropped my head.

"Oh. I didn't mean to cause you no embarrassment. That's a real talent you got Caesar. From what I heared Miss Mandy had to bust what—three or four times—in a

fifteen minute span. I ain't tryna be forward or nothin'. I just want to know if you can

bless me like that. Don't get me wrong I likes Miss Mandy and I'm glad she give me this

here job and I ain't tryna steal her man or nothin' like that. I just need some. I just need

it stroked once or twice real good. You could call it a charity fuck. I don't care but

could you do me just one time Caesar. You just don't know how bad I needs it and I sees

the way you always be lookin' at me and I'm thinking you needs it too. Don't worry I

won't let you fall in love with it. When it's over I'll point you right on back to Miss

Mandy's arms."

Just then four braves rode up.

"Morning Caesar," Yellow Knife said.

Caesar and Yellow Knife had become close friends by this time. Caesar liked the

young man who was about the same age as himself. Like Caesar Yellow Knife knew

horse flesh and the two would spend long hours just sitting and talking about horses.

"Crooked Nose told me you were riding into the fort this morning. Thought I'd

ride in with you the first time and make sure those trappers and traders don't try and take

advantage of you. You ready to go?"

"I suppose I am," I said shooting a parting glance back at Monica who was now bending over washing and purposely exposing her assets for Caesar and the others to see.

"Have to pick up those families heading in for supplies. Should be at least twelve or thirteen other families riding along."

"No problem. I'm ready when you are," Yellow Knife said never taking his eyes off the woman still bent over.

And with that we were on our way. We rode for awhile and I had to admit this Indian Territory was one beautiful country.

"So, who is she?"

"Who is who?" I asked knowing full well who Yellow Knife was referring to.

"The girl at the stream this morning."

"Just a girl Mandy hired to help out with getting set up and the baby and all."

"Thought you told me Mandy was in love with you?"

"I did."

"Then why in heaven's name would she bring all that temptation to her own doorstep?"

I smiled.

"When you find out what makes a woman tick let me be the first to know."

"Does she tickle your fancy?"

"More than you'll know," I answered.

We'd been riding for what seemed like hours when a building rose up from the plains. Looming larger as we grew closer I wondered what prompted the U.S. government to throw up a fort here. From what I could see it held no strategic advantage and had no stream or water near. In fact, there was nothing that said put a fort here and yet here it was. I only hoped and prayed we wouldn't be met with some hostile white people.

"How do they receive you?"

I could see Yellow Knife was perplexed by my question.

"What do you mean?"

"Are they hostile whites that don't want to deal with no niggras and are only interested in the green in my hand?"

Yellow Knife smiled.

"They treat me fine but I am sure they will treat you even better."

Now I was perplexed. If there was one thing I knew and that was that soldiers were soldiers. Whether Confederate or Union they both looked at us as niggas and just because we'd crossed four states and were in some place called Indian Territory I hardly expected the reception to be any different. It didn't matter if they hunted buffalos or men soldiers were a hateful sort full of venom and bitterness.

Seeing us approach the gates to the fort swung open and I began to feel better. Once inside I was speechless. Yellow Knife and his braves were in tears as they watched the reaction of my people. Everywhere I turned there were soldiers—Black soldiers— Buffalo soldiers.

"We call them Buffalo Soldiers because their here is like that of the buffalos," Yellow Knife said seeing my surprise. Now I knew why Crooked Nose was so opposed to their being transferred. I hadn't known many niggras aside from Three Winds but as nice as these men were I was quite sure that many of them would have been right at home in Free Town.

"Yas'suh. How can I be of service my good man? Oh. Pardon my manners. I'm Lieutenant Jedidiah Poole," the tall middle-aged man said standing and saluting me from his desk before catching himself and thrusting his hand out for me to shake.

"Caesar. Caesar Augustus," I said grabbing and shaking his hand.

"I've heard a lot about you Caesar Augustus. Crooked Nose holds you in rather high regard. Said I was to treat you like nobility. Seems you left quite a lasting impression on him. Says you led close to forty thousand people here looking for a better life. Now if you'd come here right after the war I'd say you made a good choice but this is not a good time for you or Crooked Nose. With the gold rush in California the government sees you and Crooked Nose and anyone else holding land between here and California as just being in the way and a nuisance. And you know what this government does to anyone it considers a nuisance. But anyway whether you decide you're here for the short term or whether you're gonna stay and try to weather the storm is your decision. But then I'm sure you have more pressing matters than me standing here boring you with my opinion. Maybe in the coming weeks we can sit down and talk. But what is it I can do for you today?"

"Just here to pick up some supplies lieutenant," I said. The man had a powerful presence and I immediately thought of papa and Uncle Andrew.

"Okay. But if you want a fair deal I'd suggest you trade with the Indians down along the border. You'd probably get a better shake. Nothin' but crooks and cheats here. Wouldn't think about sellin' any of that herd here. And might I add that those are some of the finest horses I've ever laid eyes on. See the Comanches and Apaches. They know horses and will appreciate them.

As far as your people getting their supplies let me handle that for you. The same fellow that owns and runs the general store is the Indian agent for the fort and I need not

say where he got the money to open the general store. He trusts me. I'll get your supplies and my men will load them up. Either that or he's gonna try and cheat you and you'll get back home and be madder than a wet hen," he said grinning a big wide grin that let me know that there was more than one way to skin a cat and we were fighting the good fight every day.

I thanked him and went back out and spread the word. It was many hours later when we returned. Monica was out back by the makeshift barn taking the days wash down off the line. I glanced over and nodded.

"Soon Caesar?"

"Soon Monica," I answered.

"Looking forward to that," she said smiling before scurrying to beat the rain. I took my horse into the barn where I brushed her down and fed her as I listened to the rain pelt against the roof.

I was soaked by the time I reached the shanty thrown up to keep the rain at bay until our house was built. It wasn't much but tonight it would serve me well. Stepping in the door I found it to be warm and toasty. Mandy loved to cook and the sweet smell of cornbread greeted me but my mind was elsewhere.

"Hey sweetie."

"What's she looking forward to Caesar?"

"Who?"

"Monica. You know goddam well who I'm talking about. Monica that's who. You said 'soon' and she said 'she was looking forward to it. You know I don't share and

I'll be damn after all we've been through if I'm gonna let some lil tramp like Monica take you from me. Now you tell me what that was about and you better make it good!"

"No one could ever take me away if I didn't want to go Mandy but you can chase me away and when you do don't blame anyone but yourself."

"Oh, you make me so mad Caesar Augustus," Mandy said the tears running down her face. "All I want you to do is love me. I want you to treat me like a queen, your queen. I don't want you to see or want anyone but me. I want you to be crazy about me.

I want you to not be able to live without me. I want you not to want to breathe if I'm gone from you. That's the kind of love I want from you because that's the way I love and feel about you Caesar. Damn I just want you to want me. I don't want you to have me because it's the right thing to do because I am the mother of your child. Damn Caesar why can't you see? Why can't you just love me the way I love you."

I knew and I understood but I couldn't make it be just because she wanted it so. I loved her but I was not in love with her. Those days were long gone. Now I did what I did out of duty and responsibility and unless something inside of me changed that would have to suffice.

Still, I loved her and did not want to see her hurt. Taking her in my arms I held her and rocked her to sleep.

August 3

There's a chill in the air that only tells me that we don't have much time before winter is upon us. We are not so low on provisions that we have to worry and there is plenty of game on the plains should we suddenly run short or the winter is unseasonably harsh but still there is much work to be done.

Mother and I are going to see Crooked Nose this morning to see about going South as the lieutenant suggested to acquire provisions for the winter. Mama insisted on taking the baby much to my chagrin but there was no arguing with mama We were in the village by sunup but you would have sworn it was mid-day. Men and women bustled to and fro while children ran this way and that screaming and yelling.

Crooked Nose was in deep council with his war chiefs and I soon realized that it couldn't be anything good this early in the morning and was content to sit off to the side so as not to intrude while mama made her rounds showing off her first grandbaby as if she were home. Seeing me Crooked Nose smiled broadly before waving me over.

"My enemy is your enemy making you my friend," he said in front of his war chiefs. I wasn't sure if he were asking me or telling me. I nodded in agreement.

But what I did gather through an interpreter was that General Sheridan had set forth a campaign to move all the plains Indians onto reservations.

'The only good Indian is a dead Indian' had been Sheridan's rallying cry and soon became his legacy as he attacked and massacred Black Kettle's village.

Chief Black Kettle standing before his village was gunned down holding an American flag under the guise of a recent peace treaty signed between he and the United States.

"Now he is crossing through Indian Territory ruthlessly massacring Kiowas, Arapahos, Comanches and Apaches. It will not be long before he will attack the Northern Cheyenne.

We have not done anything to provoke these attacks but and although I feel deep sorrow and sadness for my brother Black Kettle and his people I do not want to share a similar fate and be wakened to the sound of our women and children crying and being gutted like pigs. I say we take the fight to him and show him what the Northern Cheyenne is made of. All who are in favor of taking the fight to Sheridan speak now."

A cheer of solidarity rose from the council of war chiefs.

"Are there any who oppose?"

There was much chatter in the council of chiefs and then one voice rose above them all.

"Crooked Nose knows that as my brother and friend I have always followed your lead. I have never shied away from battle and this is why I sit with you as a war chief today. But we have lived in peace with the white soldiers for many years. If we were to attack Sheridan we would be breaking the treatise and inviting Sheridan and those like him to attack us. I say we show patience and send an envoy to the great father in Washington with our concerns."

"It is true Yellow Knife. You are a great warrior and one of my most trusted friends. We have fought many a battle side-by-side and you have the respect of everyone present at this council my brother but let me ask you this. When has the great father in Washington ever cared about the Indians concerns? Sheridan is in his employ. Why do you think he is unaware and not in agreement with Sheridan? Sheridan cannot proceed on his campaign without the great father in Washington's consent." Crooked Nose commented.

"Sheridan is currently four days to the south of us and killing every Indian in his path. Even if we could send an envoy it would not reach the great father in time. But our first concern must be to protect that which is ours."

Cheers rose from the council as the war chiefs got up from the war council and made their way to their braves and readied them for battle. Crooked Nose was still talking to some of his chiefs when Yellow Knife approached.

"You know this war will not end well for the people. It will mean the end of the people. We will become a ragtag bunch of old women like Geronimo and his band who are running and hiding and starving to death in the mountains to the south. We cannot take on the government and think we can survive. There are far too many."

It was hard to argue with Yellow Knife. His reasoning was sound and I can remember papa and Uncle Andrew coming to the same conclusion and we ending up here. But I did not say anything. Both of these men were my friends and I held allegiances to both but I knew Yellow Knife's words rang with an air of truth that could not be denied but there was no alternative but to flee or be killed.

When most of the talk of war was done and the villages had been warned and were preparing for battle Cooked Nose joined me and mama in front of his lodge. It was clear from his demeanor that despite his show of strong leadership at the council of the war chiefs that he held the weight of his people on his shoulders and I felt for him. I knew that it was an unenviable position he was in and I thought of the repercussions it held for me and mine.

We had not incurred the wrath of this General Sheridan and only held a small plot of land on the very fringes of Indian Territory but if history proved correct there was little difference between our red brothers and their plight and our own.

I had not addressed the council as to my decision to join Crooked Nose but there were some decisions that a leader must make unilaterally despite opposition.

"You have come to visit at a very bad time for the people."

"My friend's enemy is our enemy," I said smiling at Crooked Nose although my insides said to leave and be clear of this latest mess.

Crooked Nose smiled as he stirred the small campfire with a branch. These were troubling times and I could feel my friend's misery and turmoil as he mulled over this latest incursion into the peace and solitude of his people.

"Leadership comes with many responsibilities. And often times we are forced to make decisions on behalf of our loved ones that don't always sit well with who we are as a person but the choices and decisions we make overrule how we feel but they must be made for the good of all. My father used to tell me that in the face of overwhelming odds sometimes it is best that we run and live to fight another day," mama said grabbing Crooked Nose's hands in her own.

He looked at mama and smiled.

"So you think my people should make haste and leave this country that is ours?"

"You are a man like us and like us we have no country that we can lay rights to. This is his country and he has given you land that he can reclaim when he sees a need to. You are not seeing this for the first time.

We too had a land that we thought was ours until he decided that it was rich in resources and could be profitable to him. And then he reclaimed it leaving us to either die trying to defend it or abandon it. That is what the white man does."

"So you think that the people should abandon our homes?"

"And stay alive to fight another day? Yes, that's what I would do if for no other reason than so Light Feather could enjoy her children and grandchildren. So, there is someone that can speak of Crooked Nose greatest chief of the Northern Cheyenne. So, the tales of this great warrior can be passed down through the generations…"

Crooked Nose was overcome with grief and the tears flowed freely from this great chiefs eyes.

"And how is that you have nothing to say my friend?"

I knew he was talking to me but I did not respond. I couldn't. We had just experienced the very same thing and I still had not, could not put it in perspective. There had been little or no choice. We had to leave—run—or be exterminated. It was that simple. We too were warriors fighting for our lives but when the writing on the wall had been plain it was the people that came first. There were no alternatives. Run or be killed.

It had long been Mexican policy to offer asylum to the Indians for guarding the border and had I known that is where I would have led my people. But unaware of this at the time we did not know and chose here only to meet with the same dilemma we had tried so hard to distance ourselves from.

"Because you are my friend I had no choice but to support you but now that we are alone I must tell you that I think you are wrong my friend. I disagree with Yellow Knife that talking to President Grant would make a difference.

The man has no malice in his heart when it comes to niggras and Indians but neither has he protected us when it comes to white settlers infringing on what is rightfully and legally ours. Now we are confronted with the idea of dying trying to protect what is ours. Still…" I said grabbing the little girl who poked me with a stick playfully despite her grandfather's admonishments. "Still, we must not forget that we are only here to

make a better world for our children and grandchildren. Take your people to Mexico so that this little girl can grow to be a strong woman."

"A strong woman who will look at her grandfather not as the great and powerful chief of the Northerner Cheyenne but as a coward who turned tail and ran… No. I think it is a more important lesson to teach the children that we are a strong people and will

fight for what is right," Crooked Nose said angrily. "I will not ask you to jeopardize your people if this is the way you feel."

"My son gave you his word. And I give you mine. Any enemy of my fried is an enemy of mine. We have to break the news to our people and after that we will be back," mama said standing now.

Following mama's lead I mounted up for the ride back. We had only been in Free Town a matter of weeks and it now seemed that this would not be our last stop. We rode in silence for a spell before mama turned to me.

"What are your thoughts my son?"

"My thoughts are many mother. If only father and Uncle Andrew were here."

"But they are not and so you must ask yourself what would they do."

"I do believe that we owe Crooked Nose our allegiance but I hate to be the one to tell our people that we are to take up arms again and leave our homes."

"You are a leader of men and with that goes the unenviable duty of being the bearer of troubling news that they may not be willing to accept gracefully. Be prepared for that and do what is best for the general welfare of all."

"Do I have a choice?"

"No son. I'm afraid you don't."

Not another word was said the remainder of the ride. A morning ride with mother had turned into another hardship in the making.

Entering the lean to we called home Mandy's smile quickly disappeared.

"What's wrong sweetie? Is everything okay?"

When I'd finished Mandy sat there speechless.

"What can I do? Do you want me to have the seniors pack?"

"No. Sheridan's army is four days march from here. I'm leaving troops here to protect Free Town. If things however don't go well I'll get word back."

"My God! Will there never be any peace for the niggra?"

I left her there crying. Truth was I wondered the same thing.

Mama and Aunt Petunia called the people together. A large square in the center of Free Town was our meeting place and I stood before thousands of our folks and shared the news.

"Caesar Augustus this is not Three Winds and you nor your people own this land. You can no longer make decisions for us. Too many have already died by your leadership. And now you bring us here and tell us that we must leave again. No longer is that your decision to make. President Lincoln declared us free and that does not mean we will readily turn ova one massa for another."

Aunt Petunia who had been quiet and out of site for the entire time we had been in Free Town now spoke up.

"Mr. Man I'm not sure this is the right time to make a name for yourself or to try and wrestle power from my nephew. I cannot pretend to know your motivation but do not be so short-sighted as to know why we claim Free Town today. It is because Crooked Nose gave us safe passage and allotted this land which is his.

Now he is being displaced just as we were and he has asked our help. Politics can be discussed at a later date."

"No disrespect Miss Petunia but we are tired of fighting and dying and now you are asking us to once again give our men to a fight which is not even ours."

"As a former slave you should be well aware of how it feels to be thought of as nothing and having no say in matters which directly affect you. The U.S. government sees little difference between me and my red brothers. If he can be displaced from his land then what's to say the same can't be done to us here in Free Town? No. This is not the red man's fight. This is our fight."

Mama stood up then. I knew she was angry but the last thing I needed her to do was to cause any more dissension. But you know mama. Shoot now. Think later.

"I'd just like to address Mr. Man before we get underway. Mr. Man I heard no opposition on Three Winds when my brother and husband were beaten and berated by the colonel. I never heard any opposition when they gave you the know-how so you and your family could become fairly comfortable. I never heard you complain when my son led you on raids that made you a wealthy man. So, why am I hearing something from you now when he calls on you to be of service? Mr. Man I think it's time you anteed up and threw in. If you still have those concerns when you return I can only hope that you will bring them to me so I may address them."

What I knew of Man came from Mandy and I didn't deem him to be the brightest fox in the den and I could only imagine what a discussion with mama could mean.

An hour later, close to a thousand men dressed in our all black uniforms and close to three hundred women, all good with a rifle left from Free Town. We met Crooked Nose's braves some ten miles down the road. Aunt Petunia and mama took control of their units while Michael, Joshua's oldest son led the remainder.

Crooked Nose was genuinely happy to see us but never let on.

"From what my braves tell me Sheridan has no more than a regiment of about twelve hundred men on a forced march directly towards us. Says they have been travelling a day and a half without sleep hoping to catch us by surprise."

"With your braves and our troops outnumbering him six-to-one I think he will be the one surprised," Mama said before wheeling her horse around and galloping to see what all the commotion was about in the ranks.

"That mother of yours is some woman. She seems to relish a good fight," he grinned. "We need more with her spirit."

"It's all she's ever known."

"How did your people take the news?"

"They are disappointed and saddened by this latest turn of events but they're resilient. There were those that protested and I only fear for them. Mama said she would deal with them when she got back."

"That's not a good omen."

"Not good at all," I agreed. "Any word on how far away Sheridan's army is?"

"No more than a day away?"

"Then let me get back with my people. I will see you soon my friend."

Not long after I got back than Crooked Nose stopped the column which stretched close to a mile and a half to water the horses and rest. After checking the men and finding them in pretty good spirits I was surprised to find Celeste among those women who had joined us to fight.

"Ms. Greene."

"Why the sudden formality Caesar?"

"Just surprised to find you in attendance," I admitted.

"C'mon Caesar. Were you not listening to Fiona? We are so blessed thanks in large part to your family and its guidance. You know before I got to Three Winds I had no goals, no aspirations, no hope but I ran into this group of Black folks that refused to be denied and after awhile I too took on that same attitude and am proud of all that I have become and it's thanks to them. So, when the time comes when they say they need me who am I to say no?"

I smiled.

"I understand. You be safe. You hear?" I said dashing off. I did understand but this was a fight that didn't have to be fought. We could have just as easily circumvented Sheridan and fled to Mexico and avoided the senseless bloodshed and tears that would follow but I had given my allegiance when things hadn't exactly been in our favor and now it was time to pay the piper but it felt more like offering the lambs up for the slaughter. I needed to get away with my thoughts, with my guilt, with my discontent. Finding a dying weeping willow by a rambling brook I sat.

"Don't ever second guess yourself Caesar. You are a good shepherd. A good shepherd always considers his flock before he considers himself. May I sit down?"

The last person I expected to see was Monica.

"By all means."

"You know I've been watching you Caesar and you're a young man that has the weight of the world on his shoulders. You're growing old before your time. I know your legacy and I know expectations are high but you are not solely responsible for the inhabitants of Free Town. A good deal of the responsibility for their lives remains with them."

I looked at this woman again. It was surprising that one so young could be so wise.

"I don't know how this affair will turn out but if I were you the first thing I would do when I got back would be to set up a general election. I think that asshole Man was right to a degree but that's only because I worry about you Caesar. You should allow the people to elect a town council and a mayor to relieve you of all the decision making and relieve you of some of the burden."

I didn't say anything but I'd had the same thoughts on more than one occasion on the journey west.

"What?! You look surprised," Monica said smiling. "Didn't know I had a thought up there did you? You thought I was just another pretty face who'd you'd eventually poke when you got around to it didn't you?" Monica said laughing now. "Sorry. You got

the wrong gal this time. But and I don't know if it's a good time to tell you this but then what better time. And I want you to know that I have no ulterior motives and Miss Mandy is in no way at fault but Man is trying to have all that's yours beginning with Miss Mandy. It's almost as if he knows when you're going to be away from the ranch. She has done everything but shoot him and he still shows up. It's almost as if he has something on her. And you saw the way he acted in the town meeting. All I'm saying is be careful Caesar. Not everyone has your best interest at heart," and with that Monica got up and headed toward her horse.

"Can you shoot?"

"The best shot on the O'Reilly Place."

So, that's where she was from. I knew she looked somehow familiar like some face out of the past. Still, I couldn't place her. And why had she chosen to tell me this. He knew women could be treacherous with motives all their own and Monica appeared no different. Why had she just shown up? Was she trying to take Mandy's place?

"Mind if I ask you something Monica?"

She smiled as if she'd knew I'd have questions.

"Sure. But if it's about our getting intimate I don't think this is the time?" she said grinning at me as she swung her leg over the saddle.

That was the last thing on my mind although I have to admit that her sharp mind made her even more attractive and me just a tad bit curious.

"You're right. I think any mention of intimacy would be quite inappropriate in lieu of our present situation. No my concern is why you feel so adamant about my welfare when you hardly know me?"

"I know you better than you think Caesar Augustus," she said smiling before riding off to join the others.

Her last remark left me questioning, wondering but there was no time for that right now. The troops were pulling out. The next time we would rest would be right prior to meeting Sheridan.

I had never pushed as hard as Crooked Nose pushed us. The Cheyenne were known for their horsemanship and I was surprised at how long these men could stay in their saddles without a break and my boys showed their resolve by keeping up.

That day exhausted we bedded down. The night was cold and I had a hard time sleeping although most if not all of our troops seemed to have no problem. Staring up at

the sky I considered Monica's words. Why was Man hanging around the ranch when I wasn't there and why hadn't Mandy told me of his comings and goings? What did he have on her and what was she trying to hide? There had never been any secrets between them.

"Cold night isn't it?"

"That it is."

"Mind if I snuggle up next to you?"

I lifted the covers up and made room as she threw her own blanket over mine before lying down. She was warm and felt good as she stuck her butt in my groin area. I immediately felt myself growing erect.

"Down Caesar. Soon but this is not the time."

I immediately relaxed and again wondered what her angle was. There would be plenty of time to worry about that but I was exhausted after the day's pronouncement and soon was fast asleep.

August 4

It was even colder the next morning when I awoke. Monica was gone and as was their custom the Cherokee braves were already up and saddling their horses when I awoke. Grabbing some beef jerky and a cup of black coffee I walked the camp checking the overall morale and readiness of my troops.

All were in a good frame of mind and many almost seemed anxious for battle. An hour later after meeting with mama, Aunt Petunia, Crooked Nose and some of his war chiefs we decided on a three pronged attack with Crooked Nose's braves coming in a three stage frontal attack while mama and Michael would hit them from the right flank and auntie would hit them from the left. I was to rest that day and take my unit in that night to harass them when they were asleep. The Akansas River with its swift flowing current would serve as the backdrop giving Sheridan and his men no escape route. After the war council everyone felt better about our undertaking and in less than a half an hour we were again on the move.

My thoughts continually surrounded the women and I wondered if bringing them hadn't been an error in judgment on my part. We already outnumbered Sheridan by six to one so there really was no need for them.

Three hours later we encountered Sheridan moving at a forced march up the Arkansas. We eased into position surrounding him on three sides just as planned with the Arkansas to his back. We must have been a sight to see as upon seeing us twenty or thirty of his troops broke rank and fled to us seeking mercy. Sheridan had half of them shot in the back. I suppose he considered them deserters. I considered them smart enough to recognize the inevitable and those that were lucky enough to escape Sheridan's bullets were taken as prisoners of war.

Crooked Nose saw what we all did. Sheridan was pinned down, outnumbered with no possible means of escape. And although he insisted on riding into the jaws of the lion I eventually was able to get through to my friend.

"There is no reason to rush him. He knows without a shot being fired that he is defeated. Let us not exacerbate the situation. He is pinned down with nowhere to go. If we never to fire a shot he and his men will starve to death. There is no need to kick him when he is down. He knows he is a defeated man."

"This man is the same man that said the only good Indian is a dead Indian. This is the same man that massacred Black Kettle under a flag of truce. This man Sheridan does not deserve to be alive."

"I agree my friend but tell him that. Do not send your braves down there to count coup and die in the face of his howitzers. Do not let one man die. He is not worth you losing a good

brave, a husband, a father. Be patient my brother and allow me and my men to show you a different type of warfare, one that will inflict casualties and eliminate the fire in the eyes of the enemy. It took mama, auntie and me to convince Crooked Nose to sit back and show some restraint to this proud warrior but all of us had seen enough killing and dying not to want to see anymore.

It was Yellow Knife's idea to send an envoy to sit down with Sheridan but each time he attempted to send one of his braves under the white flag of truce he was sent scurrying back by Sheridan's marksmen.

"What kind of man is this who is faced with the inevitable and chooses to die when there is an alternative," Crooked Nose asked me.

"I cannot answer that but this I will tell you. If we kill those soldiers they will chase us until the ends of the earth and killed all of us. Let us walk away from this day without young men on either side dying and live to tell our children how we defeated the soldiers without a single shot being fired. When this day is done let us give him time to go back to the great father and tell him more lies of tens of thousands of Blacks and Indians plotting to take over his United States. And in the meantime we will take our families and travel to peace and tranquility in the land called Mexico which welcomes us openly."

"You are a dreamer my friend but I will let you try it your way despite my braves being angry. Then if it doesn't work we will do it my way. Agreed?"

"Agreed. If by tomorrow morning Sheridan still refuses to meet with us then by all means have a go at it."

Aside from an occasional brave riding into arms range of the 7th Cavalry there were no other heroics and Sheridan seemed content enough to stand pat. Then again what other choice did he have?

My elite squad was ready though decimated by the battles at Three Winds. Originally consisting of two hundred troops our ranks had been decimated and we now stood but a hundred and sixty. Yet, we were in tip top shape and ready to go.

At around four I made my rounds to make sure everyone was okay and in place. Seeing that it was I retreated to an outlying area of the camp threw my blanket and saddle down and tried to rest up before the night's raid.

"Mind if I sit?"

I recognized the voice immediately and a warm feeling went through me.

"You already know the answer to that Monica. I don't know why you would even bother to ask," I stated smiling. "I like your company. For some reason you intrigue me but tell me this how is it that you always seem to know where to find me?"

"I never leave you," she said smiling and dragging an old log over to within inches of where I was lying down.

"And what is that supposed to mean."

"Exactly that. I never let you out of my sight."

"Is that right?"

"Yes. I guess I'm sorta like your fairy godmother."

"So you take care of me?"

"I guess you could say that?"

"Then why do I feel that you're somehow not doing your job."

"All things in time Caesar."

"Is that like 'soon'?"

"Similar," Monica said blushing and exposing her dimples. "So, what's the plan?"

"Going to 'cause a distraction and then go in and kidnap Sheridan and some of his officers and bring 'em back and sit down and proceed with peace talks. This should last the better part of a week. I've already sent a courier back. They should be loading up now and on

the road by no later than tomorrow morning. They should be passing within ten miles of us in two days on the way to Mexico."

"Oh that's good. That's really good. That's genius Caesar. I may just have to give you some one day."

"You promise?"

"Mind if I lay down here next to you?"

"Only if you slide under the cover with me."

"Fraid I can't oblige you today sweetheart."

"Is it something I did?"

"Quite to the contrary. I think it's everything you're doing," Monica grinned before turning her back towards me and closing her eyes.

It was early evening when he awoke. Monica was nowhere to be found but he was sure she had him in her sights as he moved to the rendezvous point to meet with his men. There were only six in the party when he stopped by Crooked Nose's teepee.

"This is your war party?" Crooked Nose laughed. "Let me tell my braves we will be going in in the morning," he said chuckling again. "I wish you luck my friend."

He then stopped on the right flank and spoke with his aunt who guaranteed that everything was in order.

"Did you get the uniforms?"

"Everything is as you requested," she said leading he and Joshua's three remaining sons to a small clearing not far from her command post. In the clearing tied to an old sycamore were three of Sheridan's soldiers sitting there nude.

"The uniforms?"

"The uniforms. Right," Aunt Petunia said going over to a wooden chest and pulling the uniforms out. "These gentlemen were nice enough to disrobe before you arrived so you wouldn't have to wait," she said smiling and handing me the uniforms. I handed the uniforms to Joshua's boys and waited with auntie while they put on the soldiers clothing.

It was the happiest I'd seen Aunt P. since she'd left Three Winds. Mama said she was sad and grieving so we left her alone to work things out. But leading her men she seemed to garner the spirit of the aunt I used to know and I knew Crooked Nose's braves weren't the only ones dying to face Sheridan's troops.

"Once you get him out of there I wouldn't be opposed to cleaning up the leftovers nephew," she said smiling devilishly and winking at me.

"I'll let you know auntie," I said grinning at her.

Along with Joshua's sons and two other men I selected specifically for the task we escorted them to the perimeter of Sheridan's camp where we laid down in the grass to provide cover fire should they run into trouble on their exit. Twenty minutes later the three exited the camp the same way they had come in and we slipped through Aunt Petunia's stronghold and back to the main camp.

"Send the wine down," I commanded.

Moments later five buckboards each carrying eight kegs of wine; four of which were tainted with poison were sent down to Sheridan's men who after having forced marched the last couple of hundred miles were exhausted and in dire need of some rest and relaxation.

The soldiers greedily devoured the wine and could be heard screaming in pain soon after. The battle was all but over now but one of Caesar's saving graces was his patience and so after making sure Sheridan was securely placed under a twenty four watch he took his leave in search of the new and brightest star in his life. Monica. After making the rounds and making sure everything was in order he sent word to Crooked Nose that he had returned to camp and would meet him and the war council in the morning.

Once this was done he made his way back to the quiet little grove she'd found him at earlier. He lay there staring up at the stars and considered their next move. His eyes grew weary and when she did not appear he closed them one last time.

August 5

I didn't realize how tired I was. I suppose the sheer anxiety of the whole undertaking has taken its toll. Today is just the beginning. We have Sheridan under wraps and having him in our custody and his troops under siege guarantees safe passage for our people. This may be the hardest part. We simply wait.

This morning I will present Sheridan to Crooked Nose as promised to avoid the slaughter of Sheridan's troops but I have no idea what plans Cooked Nose has in store for General Sheridan other than to talk to him as an equal and a leader of men. Me? I have no interest at all in knowing what Sheridan thinks. A man that states that the only good Indian is a dead Indian is not worthy of my attention. He serves a purpose and will insure the passing of my people into Mexico. After that I have no use for him.

The war council was already gathered when I arrived with my men and the general as my prisoner. Crooked Nose stood and stared at me for what seemed like forever. He was speechless. He then turned to his chiefs many of which I am sure objected to my mere presence at their war council.

"And without a brave dying," he boasted before embracing me. "And without a brave being killed and without a shot fired. Did any of you hear a shot fired in the night? I did not hear a shot fired."

The other chiefs sat speechless as well. Well that is except for Yellow Knife who beamed with pride almost as if he were the one responsible for General Sheridan's capture. Most of the chiefs at the war council were ecstatic about this latest progression and embraced me as well and there was much talk now concerning the fate of the general but not I. I had with his capture provided my people with safe passage. Free Town and my people were now only hours away from our campsite and would be passing by later today.

With Sheridan and his regiment now being held under siege—well at least those—still able to soldier I knew their journey would be that much easier. In a day or two we would join them and hopefully be out of the country before Sheridan could reach Fort Sill for reinforcements.

Now was the difficult part and I did not take part in this council choosing to sit aside with mama and auntie to listen to the questions and answers provided by General Sheridan. From the comments I heard attributed to him I did not like him and could not imagine what he could possibly say that might endear him to me. I believe Crooked Nose was curious to know what

type of man could kill women and children. But I had witnessed white men doing this with no remorse in Mississippi. These men did not recognize us for being human beings and usually had little or no remorse until they learned of their fate. I was only curious as to how he would appear in lieu of his own fate. It didn't take long to find out.

I had his restraints removed and seated across from the chiefs but this was Crooked Nose's show as he stared at Sheridan for what seemed like forever. I knew my friend was trying to let his anger subside somewhat before he spoke. He, after all, represented his people and wanted to give an unemotional and tepid response to Sheridan's atrocities. There was no need to glorify his inhumanness or incite his own people to act irrationally and emotionally.

Caesar knew that Crooked Nose had to be careful or the deaths of eight hundred U.S. soldiers under Sheridan's command would be massacred. The people were angry. They were angry that once again they were being forced to give up their lands. They were angry because this man—this General Sheridan—had massacred their cousins and nephews. They were angry because he was now on his way to do the same to them. And they were angry because in his own words 'the only good Indian was a dead Indian'.

"General Sheridan they tell me that you are a great warrior chief. I have long waited for you and I to sit down and talk as great warrior chiefs do. But you refused my requests"

"I see no great warrior chiefs," Sheridan said matter-of-factly before spitting out a wad of tobacco.

"Perhaps you do not know what it takes to be a great warrior chief. Maybe all that I hear about the great General Sheridan are all children's tales so I will tell you what makes a great warrior chief. A great warrior chief leads. He is a leader among his people and not just in times of battle but when there is no war. You see all these men before you general? These men are all great warrior chiefs. When there is battle these men lead their men. They are the first to confront the enemy because they lead them into the battle. They do not sit high on a bluff and stare though a looking glass before sending men to their death. I do not think you are a great war chief."

Crooked Nose paused and stared at the ground and I knew he was gathering his thoughts.

"So, I guess I can put my mind at ease after having sat across from you. And I think I am right when I say that you are no great chief."

"Why you red savage son-of-a-bitch," Sheridan yelled. "How dare you speak to me like that. Why I'll have you hanged."

Several of Cooked Nose's braves rose quickly, knives drawn only waiting a nod from Crooked Nose to slash this white man's throat. Waving them away Crooked Nose smiled at Sheridan.

"Most of my chiefs would agree that you are no great war chief. The battles that we know about we hear that you send your men to fight against old women and children. What kind of chief sends his men against old women and children? No. I think the better question is not are you a great chief but are you a man."

The hatred burned in Sheridan's eyes.

"Who are you to ask me such questions? Do you know who I am?"

"Yes, I am quite aware of who you are. You are the great chief of the 7th Cavalry who now sits before me Crooked Nose the great chief of the Northern Cheyenne who has captured you and laid waste to your regiment without a single shot having been fired."

"When I am finished there will not be a single Indian left on these plains."

"Perhaps you have not grasped the gravity of your situation but I think you are already finished general."

Everyone laughed as Crooked Nose stood up.

"There is nothing to learn from this man. He is no great leader. This man is a fool."

Mama and I laughed. I stood and approached the general along with several of my men. Crooked Nose now stood before us. He was deeply saddened by the responses he got from this man they touted as being one of the greatest Civil War generals.

"He has nothing to offer but hate and of that I have enough. I do not need any more hate. From what I see he has nothing else to offer."

"I did not know why you would expect any more?" mama said quite matter-of-factly. There is no thought process. He is married to his convictions that only good white men should prosper from this land and his driving force is hate. We are the only thing standing between them inheriting the earth and therefore we must be driven aside. That is what motivates him to live. Nothing else. We have seen it before."

This seemed to sadden Crooked Nose even more.

"Did you get word to your people?"

"Yes they ride with your people. They are well on their way. I will send scouts to see if they are close. I want to leave this place as soon as I can. Some of my chiefs have decided to stay and fight. They say they will fight to keep this land that is rightfully theirs but most of the people have chosen to go."

"That is because Crooked Nose great chief of the Northern Cheyenne leads them to the Promised Land where opportunity awaits them," I said smiling.

"Let's go upriver some my friend once you have checked on your people and see what the great Arkansas can offer up for dinner."

"Sounds good my friend. We've done well today," I noted. "I don't think we'll have to worry about soldiers patrolling. I think we have Fort Sill pretty much occupied down by the river. I had my men go into Sheridan's camp and relieve them of their arms. I don't believe they'll be needing them. We got about ten or twelve wagons of army issued automatic carbines. They're all new and in working order. Also picked up their big guns and artillery. Think they'll come in handy when we get where we're going. Figure we can use them to barter with should food stuffs run low this winter. All in all we're going to be hard pressed to get up and running before winter steps in."

"This is good Caesar. I think I will make you my second in command."

"That would be an honor but please do not tell anyone else about my promotion. I don't think some of your up and coming braves will be too happy about my rapid rise."

We laughed and parted ways and made our rounds. Unlike Crooked Nose's braves my men were happy not to have had to fire a shot and most if not all were in a pretty good mood despite having to be uprooted again.

"What's the plan Caesar?"

"Just bidin' our time. Waiting for the wagon train to get a few days head start before we pull out. We're gonna pull up the rear and make sure the general and his men don't try anything."

"With no guns Caesar? And no clothes?"

"No clothes?" I asked.

"Yes your Aunt Petunia had us strip the troops when we confiscated their weapons. Said there was no worse humiliation than stripping a soldier and having him have to retreat home naked. Said we could sell their clothes and may need them in case we ran into any soldiers on the way to Mexico."

I had to drop my head and smile when I heard this.

"Okay. Well, I'm just checking on you. We're going to hold our position here for a couple of days before we pull out."

"Two days! My God man what are we supposed to do for the next two days?"

"If I were you Boston I'd get all the rest I can get. You know Chalotte and them younguns is just waitin' on you," I laughed.

"Guess you're right. Didn't think about it like that," Boston said his face growing grim at the mere thought of his overbearing wife and his seven children.

Mama and Aunt Petunia and a few of the other women occupied themselves with washing the soldier's uniforms and preparing food for the troops. Seeing that all was well I set out to find Crooked Nose. Finding him we walked close to a mile or so until we had come to a place where the land intruded part way across the river. Walking out to the edge of the inlet we sat and cast our lines. The day was beautiful with the sun warming us but not too warm to be uncomfortable.

Sitting there with my friend I finally had a chance to breathe when suddenly a shot rang out and I could feel it as it brushed by my ear and then a second shot. I jumped on Crooked Nose until the shots ceased. And there where only seconds before there had been peace and quiet there arose a clatter from the thicket. Turning to see what all the commotion was about I caught eye of four or five of Crooked Nose's braves emerging from the thicket with Man in their clutches.

"Who is this man?"

"He's one of mine. I don't think you were in any danger. I'm pretty sure he was aiming for me."

Man had been shot in his attempts to kill me.

"I've been shot man. Have you no mercy Caesar?!" Man shouted at me. I ignored the blood running from his leg and continued speaking to the chief.

"This is one of my soldiers. I believe he has some problem with me although I am not quite sure what it is. Who can I thank for saving my life?" I said to Crooked Nose's braves who in turned pointed to thick grove of trees in the distance.

"The shot came from over there," they said in unison.

I glanced to where they pointed and could see a tall, thin figure emerging from the grove of trees. Coming closer I could make out Monica's fine brown frame.

"Never happier to see someone in my life," I said grabbing and hugging her tightly.

"He's been following you around the camp for the last couple of days. I kinda figured he was up to no good."

"Would you tell Aunt Petunia and ask her to put him under lock and key. Whatever you do don't give him to mama or tell her anything about what just happened."

"No problem."

"And thank you again, Monica."

"It's my job and my duty," she commented as she mounted her horse and followed Crooked Nose's braves.

The girl was an enigma to him. Who was she? Where did she come from? He knew no more about her than he did what had made Man so angry that he wanted to kill him. But he did not care at that moment. He was just glad that she'd been there.

"And to think we thought we were getting away from it all to do a little fishing," Crooked Nose said smiling and patting me o he back for reassurance. And I was just glad I hadn't chosen man for a sniper unit.

August 6th

There is a steady drizzle coming down and the camp is unusually quiet this morning. I can't say I am unhappy about this latest turn of events. The camp is anxious to move out but the rain has slowed everything to a standstill and seems to have put a damper on things. The men seem content to stay in their pup tents if not on duty.

I spent a good deal of the morning in Celeste's company.

"I am just so glad that I wasn't forced to take a life," she confessed to me. "And I am so glad that you took responsibility and had the wherewithal to devise a better plan than your friend Crooked Nose."

I did not respond but let her go on.

"We are all so very proud of you Caesar. I am only hoping that there will come a day that we will not have to resort to violence to resolve our differences."

"You and I both Celeste. You know I can remember back listening to papa recollecting on the wars he fought at Three Winds following emancipation and I couldn't

wait to join the fight. It was all so glorious then. But that grew old quick and came to a crashing end when the bloodshed started getting closer to home and ended when I saw Benjy and Buck die under my watch. If I ever have to fight in another battle it will be far too soon."

"You know there will come a day when land disputes arise and all we will do is send our lawyer to represent us and let the courts work out the dispute instead of men seeing who has the biggest gun and killing each other."

"And that will be a very good day for all of us."

"Which is why our first priority when we get settled is to build schools and teach our children the laws of the land so they can defend themselves legally."

"I am looking forward to those days."

"You know your cousin should be returning from Boston any day now. He may even be with the wagon train. They say he has his law degree now and can practice when he arrives here. He can represent us legally now."

"You're speaking of Jojo I presume?"

"Why yes silly. Who else?"

"I see. So, are you two planning on marrying when he returns?"

"I'm sure he would like to think so but my heart has always been with someone else. And then there's my career. I have so much to do before I can even think of

marrying anyone. So, don't you worry your lil head sweetheart. I'm not marrying him or anyone else right about now but when that time comes you know you'll always be my first choice love."

"That's comforting to know."

"I thought you'd like that. But don't know you know that would be extremely difficult in your present situation."

"Never you mind that. My situation is tenuous and only a temporary situation at best."

"So, you say. I suggest you do something quickly though for your sake. Her lover may not miss next time."

Her lover? How was it I was always the last to know? First Monica and now Celeste and I knew nothing. I made my leave feeling somewhat betwixt. I knew I still had a place in Celeste's heart and yet I was unnerved by the fact that things had been taking place in plain sight and yet without me knowing it between Man and Mandy. And if anyone had the answers it was Monica. I immediately went in search of her.

It wasn't until early evening before I found her with the other women upriver.

"May I have a word with you Monica?"

"Why certainly Caesar... In fact I was just about to come and find you. I'm afraid I have some very disturbing news."

"Is there somewhere we can go and talk privately?"

"Sure. Let's walk."

We walked away from the river and the other women now bathing and swimming and passing the evening.

"Last night when I took Man to your Aunt Petunia we had quite an interesting conversation. Seems the young man was or should I say is in love with Mandy. He made it known to her in every way he possibly could. Seems she led him on and when he became persistent she let him know that it was virtually impossible since she was married to Buck. What he didn't realize was that Mandy was in love with you. Anyway, she made it seem that the only way they could move forward is if Buck was out of the way so he went to them white boys and told them that Buck was the ringleader of the soldiers at Three Winds. He gave away the whole plot and cut one of the tendons of Buck's horse leaving him partially crippled. That's how they caught Buck and killed him."

"So, Mandy is really the one responsible for Buck's death?"

"It appears that way."

"And if you don't mind me asking how did you get him to open up and confess?"

"I wish I could take responsibility but in all honesty it was your Aunt Petunia who drove the nail into the coffin."

"Is he alive?"

"Yes. But like I told her she would have made one hell of a carpenter."

"Why do you say that?"

"Well after nailing that first nail into Mr. Man all she had to do was pick up the hammer and the rest just fell neatly into place."

"Where is he now?"

"She has him under house arrest. Funny thing though she told me the same thing you told me."

"And what's that?"

"Not to mention a word to your mama. Why is that Caesar?"

"Everyone knows mama and no one wants to be responsible for another murder. Mama wouldn't have given him time to confess. She has little to no patience and if you

even think about causing harm to a member of her family you might as well count your days numbered."

"I see. Well, don't let on you know anything. She asked me not to mention anything. She seems to think you have too much on your shoulders as it is."

"Well, Monica I'm not quite sure what to think or who made you my guardian angel but I do want to thank you for being there for me."

"Why can't I just be one of God's children working on the side of right with no motive attached?"

"You very well could be but then when you add with no motive attached that makes me leery but you are different than anyone I've come to know thus far." Caesar said walking away.

When I returned to camp I found Yellow Knife, mama and auntie waiting for me.

"Crooke Nose wants you to know that our people have passed us close to three hours ago. He said we can leave once you feel they have a sizeable lead and are safe."

"And what do you think my friend?"

"I would say that we should leave tomorrow to give us a good head start and then leave about a hundred braves and troops to keep them pinned down another day before they leave."

It was a good plan and I told him so. He left feeling as though he had played an integral part in our escape and safety. It was important to keep his allegiance since his

band of Cheyenne aside from Crooked Nose was the largest with him commanding close to a thousand braves. He was also my friend and closest ally I had with the Cheyenne aside from Crooked Nose who was feeling the impact from many of his chiefs for taking me into his confidence. An hour later I received news from Crooked Nose saying he concurred with the plan for our departure.

I then found a quiet place away from the camp to rest and prepare for tomorrow's journey. All seemed to be going as well as could be expected and I knew there was little more I could do at this juncture and so I closed my eyes. I had just fallen off to sleep when I heard noise from the woods behind me.

After the episode with Man taking a shot at me I have to admit I slept with one eye open and my Colt .45 by my side. But I knew this was no assassin as they hardly tried to mask their approach. Still I lay poised holding my gun cocked as the intruder steadily approached my campsite.

I soon recognized the figure approaching me. Tall and lithe Monica approached her black boots giving rise to her shapely calves. I was relieved and thought back to our earlier meeting.

"Monica I must apologize for our earlier meeting."

"No need for an apology Caesar although it's funny that you always seem to be a bit more receptive when we meet at night," she said smiling and putting her rifle down next to me before throwing her blanket down over me and climbing under it.

"So, we are leaving tomorrow?"

"Yes ma'am."

Her body now entangled with mine was hard and firm and as before I felt an erection beginning to evolve. Turning to me she said.

"If it is to happen it will but you know as well as I do that there are too many obstacles before us to give in to our carnal wants and desires."

"Carnal wants and desires?" I questioned. "Your vocabulary is quite extensive. I was not aware that they had schools on the O'Reilly Place."

"They didn't although you're right. I was sent North when I was twelve years old or thirteen to Oberlin College in Ohio. There I studied and taught 'til I received a letter from my grandfather telling me I was needed here to teach. So, I returned to find everything in an uproar."

"I knew there was something different."

"There's nothing any different about me than anyone else here aside from my perceptions. Sometimes I see things a might different than everyone else."

"They say your perceptions are your reality. And perhaps that's what separates you from most of our people."

"And how would you know that Caesar? My allure for you is superficial. To you my whole appeal is the fact that I'm attractive woman that you have yet to bed down. To me I'm no more than another notch on your belt."

"How can you say that?"

"Easily since you have not taken the time to get to know me."

"I wish I could argue your point but I am ashamed to admit you're right. How do I apologize?"

"By taking the time to get to know me. You may like what you find."

"You're like a spirit on the tail of the winds in and out so rapidly it is difficult to corner you for a conversation and then before you're gone again. How am I to get to know you?"

"I didn't say it would be easy," Monica said smiling. "But then most things worth having don't come gift wrapped. You have to work for them. Good night Caesar."

"So, what you're telling me is that if I want you I have to work for you?"

"Good night Caesar. We have a long day ahead of us."

August 7th

Monica wasn't wrong about it being a long day. I awoke to the sounds of screaming coming from Crooked Nose's camp and immediately made my way to the noise to see what was wrong. What could possibly be wrong? All the men had to do was put their meager belongings together and be ready to ride. And from what I could gather we had done so and were only waiting for y command to be on our way.

The same cannot be said for Crooked Nose's camp, which to be fair, was made up of several roving bands that had been summoned to ward off government troops who had now begun intruding on their lands. It seems sometime just before sunup several braves from Santanta's band had entered Sheridan's camp to rummage through the soldier's belongings to see if they could find some items of value. Instead they found four officer's wives being transported by Sheridan to Fort Arbuckle where they were to meet with their husbands.

The braves had brought them back as prisoners or should we more aptly describe them as the spoils of war. Now here was Santanta arguing with Yellow Knife and Crooked Nose.

"What Santanta does not understand is that my friend Caesar has risked his life to save all of us. When we end this march we will be in a new country with a new beginning. Soldiers will not cross into Mexico as we have not committed any crime other

than to humiliate the white soldiers so intent on destroying us. We have lost no braves and they have lost no troops. But taking these women will be tantamount to killing every last one of Sheridan's men and they will come into Mexico with the intent once again of killing all of us. We do not need to bring this upon our women and children. Taking these women would be putting our women and children at risk."

"And have you forgotten what these same men did to our brother Black Kettle and his people?"

"No. I have not forgotten. But I will ask you as I asked General Sheridan. What great war chief makes women and children a part of his battle? What man involves women in his battles? Return the women to their camp and let us be on our way."

Crooked Nose was right but the anger and bitterness had long ago festered in Santanta and he could no longer see things clearly.

By now auntie and mama had their troops mounted and we stood idly by while the chiefs argued on. My two hundred elite moved to the front of the procession and now stood by my side. Waving my hand they dismounted. Signaling them once again they placed their hands on their sabers.

"So, now you would let your niggras fight your battles Crooked Nose?"

"You did not say that when the niggras brought you Sheridan but to make things perfectly clear I have not asked anyone to fight my battles but not only do you risk our lives but the lives of these people seeking a land free of danger. Think of the killing you would bring to them for the sake of four white women."

"I believe my friend Crooked Nose has grown soft in his attempts to get along with the whites. How can you even let this niggra sit at our war council as if he were a great war chief? Yes, I believe Crooked Nose has grown soft."

"Why do you insult my friend Santanta? Is it because he has outshone you in battle? Caesar is one of the greatest war chiefs I know."

"And what battle has he outshone Santanta in?"

"The battle we have just won. I have not known you Santanta to ever to have such a complete and resounding victory without a brave losing their life. Now return the women to their camp."

I gave the signal to my men and they returned their sabers to their scabbards and mounted up as Crooked Nose made his final decree. What I wasn't expecting was Santanta's response.

"We are keeping the women as well as our lands. We will not be riding with you but will stay here and defend what is rightfully ours. Old women run in the face of danger. There are no old women that ride with us. We are not like the niggras who bring their women to fight their battles.

Before he could finish a shot rang out and Santanta went down and mama stepped up to the crying man.

"Old women talk when there is no need for talking. Now get up and stop whining. Caesar have the women returned to their camp."

I looked Crooked Nose who had dropped his head smiling.

"Put him in my wagon so I can look after him," mama said. When it looked as those some of his braves were going to disagree mama walked up to them and said.

"My name is Fi- and I lead the second unit if you ever have a need to come looking for me. I'm easy to find. I have never professed to be a great chief like Santanta did but I take care of my people. Now mount up if you're coming with us. We need to be on our way."

I have to admit I have never been so proud of mama and not long after that we were on our way.

Four or five hours later, I noticed both the weather and landscape had changed abruptly. There was considerably less foliage now and the air was more arid. Still, the trip was surprisingly comfortable and so I made my way to find mama though I made sure I didn't bring up the shooting of Santanta and it was in fact she that brought it up.

"You know men are a funny sort. They have this thing with power and control. What is it that makes them have to be ruler and in charge of everything?"

"Wish I knew mama."

"Ya know I can remember your papa during around about the time Lincoln was considerin' endin' slavery. We was fightin' our own war in support of the Union. The council did everything to disrupt the Confederate supply wagons, aided the Underground Railroad and those slaves that decided to run. We pretty much plotted to kill every slave master that had made it intolerable for a niggra. It was a lot of killin' durin' those times. I mean a lot... More than you can imagine. They'd send out their patrols at night and we'd send out ours. They demanded that we have passes to travel and we demanded that if they didn't have a reason to be out or a specific destination then they must be chasin' niggras and were therefore condemned to death. We killed a lot of no-good, poor, white trash that made a living offa making niggras suffer and I ain't never regretted not a one of

those lives I took. 'Til this day I do believe I was doing the Lord's work. If I was wrong he will be the one to judge me when I reach the pearly gates."

"I hear you mama."

"This fool I got here in the back probably should be dead. My son risks his life and saves the lives of thousands and he wants to jeopardize all that for some pinched face white woman and he's already married three times and his homelands in jeopardy of being overrun. If I was his wife and he came home with a white woman I'd kill his ass off for sure. Only reason he's still breathing and ain't pushin' up daisies is because of the backlash it would have had on Crooked Nose. I'm pretty sure if I had killed him Crooked

Nose's people would have looked at Crooked Nose and questioned him as to how he let someone, an outsider and a niggra come in and kill family so I had mercy on Crooked Nose not Santanta. Do you understand?"

"Perhaps that's the first question you should have asked. You could have simply said Caesar do you understand what happened this morning? And I would have said yes mama and we wouldn't have had to go through that long diatribe. I swear the more I talk to you the more I think papa was a saint for just having had to endure you for all these years."

Mama laughed.

"Get outta here boy," she said. Leaning over I kissed her on the cheek. "Your father would be oh so proud of you."

"And you mama?"

"You already know," she said wiping a tear from her cheek. "Now go on git."

We rode steadily all that day and much of the next still not seeing the wagon train.

On the third day we caught up with them and I felt a sense of relief although my work seemed to double. The wagon train now extended over four miles now and the

dispersion of troops to cover it in its entirety was a job in itself and took hours to do in shoring up the places it was most vulnerable.

It was early evening on our third day before I had an opportunity to check in with my friend Crooked Nose. The worried look I had come to know so well was etched on his face.

"We are in Kiowa, Comanche, and Apache lands now and subject to attack at any time. They are no friend of the Cheyenne."

I didn't ask why. It wasn't important. What had taken place was history and my only thoughts were of getting through this unscathed.

"Tell your men to be alert. I have sent scouts out in all four directions. They are long overdue and I fear they may have been killed so tell your men to be on their toes," he said repeating the command. "We are less than two days march from Mexico but these may be the hardest two days march we have ever done. In another hour or so we will bed down for the night unless you can convince your people that it would be prudent if they can keep moving."

"I'm not sure I can demand any more from them. My troops are exhausted. And if we are to encounter any resistance I think they will serve better if they are fully rested."

"Then let us keep on for another hour or so. There is a box canyon up ahead if my memory serves me right and we can hole up there for the night. It has but one entrance that will hold us all and a narrow passageway at the entrance that will only need two men to stand guard after we are inside."

"That sounds like a plan to me and I will see you after we are all settled in."

"Where is your mother Caesar?"

"She commands the second unit about two miles back."

"Can you relieve her and ask her to come see me. I would like to thank her for this morning."

"I will do that," I said wheeling my horse around and heading off at a gallop before he called me to stop.

"Take my oldest daughter, Sonya and have her escort Fiona back," he said nodding to the beautiful woman who rode to the right of him.

I had seen her, sometimes in his company before and had shied away. Of her beauty there was little doubt. It was unnerving and although she was coy and reserved her beauty unnerved me and I often found it difficult to speak. Our relationship up until now consisted of a nod on my part and a smile on hers. Crooked Nose had obviously noticed and commented on more than one occasion.

"I don't know what's wrong but I fear she will grow old and leave me with no grandchildren. She is too picky when she cannot afford to be. Many of my braves are afraid to approach her because I am her father. Those that do she dismisses like the buffalo dismisses the flies that light upon him. She seemingly has no interest. But you would make a fine son-in-law Caesar. You are both honorable and brave. Might you have a go at it? I see the way she looks at you."

"I feel honored that you would think of me in such a way Crooked Nose but I am only a soldier. I only know of soldiering. Of women I know little."

Crooked Nose smiled.

"And she knows little of men. Perhaps you can learn together."

"Perhaps."

"I understand that she is not your kind. And I would hold nothing against you if you do not choose her but at least come to get to know her."

I agreed but had yet to say anything. Now it was Cooked Nose in lieu of the impending danger that pushed us together. And although she was an expert horseman I

slowed my horse to an easy trot with her by my side. Seeing me my men took notice and though I couldn't make out the words a steady whisper arose as we passed by.

I knew that Crooked Nose loved his oldest daughter perhaps more than he loved all of his other children so for him to offer her to me was the ultimate compliment he could assign me. I also knew that any union with Sonya would ally our two peoples and I would be forever bound to the Cheyenne. It was a smart move on Crooked Nose's part and would assure my allegiance and military help but I had enough problems and a woman, and the oldest daughter of my friend the great chief of the Northern Cheyenne was one I did not want or need. So, and although I'd picked up a good deal of the Cheyenne language I did not make conversation with this woman.

All I could think of was Uncle Andrew's words when he'd found me groping at some girl when I was a teenager. He hadn't interrupted when he found us down by the stream that day but the next day he had me sent for and I can remember his words as if they were yesterday.

'Son everything that looks good isn't good for you,' he'd admonished. "You don't step in every hole you see.'

I'd understood and took heed and those words stuck with me over the years and I could hear them now just as clearly as the day he'd said them. And despite the rumors

aside from Mandy and a couple of others I thought I was in love with at the time I had heeded his words. And that's not to say that if Monica or Celeste had given me the green light I wouldn't have indulged but the fact remains that the women I wanted did not exactly reciprocate in their want for me. But for right now Celeste and Monica were more than enough for any one man.

I was lost in deep thought when I heard the first shot and saw one of Crooked Nose's braves fall from his horse. Several more fell from their horses before the shooting ended and then just like that it was all over. I'd ordered my people to circle up the wagons but by the time they had it was all over.

Crooked Nose's braves were quick to pursue the attackers and I wondered who could have possibly ordered an attack on a wagon train of close to seventy thousand people. Our mere numbers if nothing else had to be intimidating but attack us they did killing twelve braves. Crooked Nose's braves used to these hit-and-run guerilla tactics followed the men and were back within minutes having captured two of the attackers. I rode up to my friend Crooked Nose to see how he had fared and was pleasantly surprised to see him composed despite the attack on his men.

"Set up a burial detail and have the column move forward in haste," he commanded.

His men stood in front of him with the two captives bloody and shaken. The two men or I should say boys who couldn't have been more than fourteen or fifteen were visibly shaken now. Seems they'd been out with a small hunting party when they'd come across us and in an attempt o take coup and make a name for themselves had attacked us.

"What tribe do you call yourself?" Crooked Nose asked the young boy now in front of him.

"We are Kiowa," the young boy said proudly.

"And what clan are you with?"

"I am the son of Chief Big Tree," the young man announced.

"So, you are the son of my good friend Big Tree?" Crooked Nose said looking at the young boy. "We will just see what your father thinks of your leading a raid against his friends the Northern Cheyenne. But for now you will be held as a prisoner of war until your father comes to claim you. You have killed some good men and will work for the families of those men whose lives you are responsible for taking. Take them away.

Moments later we were back on our way with Crooked Nose leaving a small burial party with a few of his most trusted braves to guard them against any further mishap.

The land had now turned into mostly desert and I wondered if our final destination posed the same terrain. My people were mostly farmers and the land did not look as if it would support anything. And aside from the rain we'd had days ago there was not a cloud in the sky.

Moving at a torrid pace Crooked Nose announced that in only a matter of hours we would be in Mexico but my men were worn out from the pace and demanded that we stop and rest.

That night we holed up in the canyon Crooked Nose had spoken of and everyone was relieved. Tomorrow we would be in Mexico and away from the United States Calvary so intent on us meeting our demise. Most of us just lay around in small groups talking and speculating on what Mexico held for us. There were a great many questions but none of which I could answer as I had no idea what this new land held for us. Some anxious members of my party went to speak with Crooked Nose's people in hopes of finding answers but the Cheyenne were not agrarians and could not help in their requests for what Mexico held for them.

Later that evening a large contingent of Kiowas of more than four or five hundred braves rode to the mouth of the canyon. It was then that I realized that this canyon was not as ideal as I thought. Relegated to this canyon we were at the mercy of any army planning on waging war against us. It was easily defensible but at the same time with us boxed in all they had to was sit and wait until we had run out of provisions. They could not attack us that was true but then they didn't have to. All they had to do was wait us out. It was a war of attrition.

It was Aunt Petunia who first recognized this and brought this to Crooked Nose's attention. Seeing the folly of his tactics Crooked Nose suggested we sleep for a few hours before moving on.

This was never more true than when a Kiowa war party led by Big Tree arrived at the mouth of the canyon demanding to speak to Crooked Nose.

"My friend I beg you at the behest of my son and my people to temper your anger when speaking to the Kiowas. Our future depends on your tact in handling this affair," mama said to Crooked Nose.

Crooked Nose laughed.

"It is funny that you should speak to me of temperance and restraint. When I take you as my fourth wife I will call you Shoots First Talks Later," he laughed before patting her on her back and walking away.

Then walking to the mouth of the canyon he pointed to two of his braves protecting the entrance and ordered them to let the Kiowa chief advance.

Once inside the canyon Cooked Nose greeted Big Tree chief of the Kiowas with open arms, hugging the old man.

"It has been many moons my friend since you and I have had a seat at the same war council or shared a good smoke. Come let us do that now."

The older man carried himself with a certain regalness seen in few men and I wondered how after all these people had been through they still had the strength and fortitude to carry themselves in such a manner.

"I guess my friend Crooked Nose knows why I am here today. I have heard great things about your exploits in my country. I hear tell that you have defeated the mighty Sheridan without a shot being fired and sent him home naked and crying like a little girl."

"This is true," Crooked Nose said. "But I do not believe that is the reason for your visit today."

"Please do not make me humble myself before you Crooked Nose. I have come to retrieve my son."

"Your son is responsible for the deaths of twelve of some of my finest braves."

"So I've heard. But he is young. You do remember when we were young?"

"Yes, I do remember when we were young and foolish and I am guessing you want me to show compassion and return your son to you?"

"Yes. I fear if you do not I will have the wrath of his mother on my head. You do remember my wife don't you?"

"Yes. I remember Black Cloud and I feel for you old man but I cannot release your boy at this time. I have twelve families who are grieving the loss of their sons, husbands, fathers and brothers. What do I tell those that are grieving their loss?"

"I don't know and I do understand my friend but think of me. The boy is my only son. Sometimes I think he takes more after his mother's side of the family when it comes to common sense but I promise you I will punish him."

"I'm sorry Big Tree. I do feel for you but I cannot let you take him but what I can do is let him work for those family's that lost their loved ones until the grieving period is over and then return him to you. I give you my word on that."

"I guess I can ask no more in lieu of the trouble and sadness he has caused your people. I thank you Crooked Nose and I am glad that we can still part as friends. I will send you some braves with the morning sun and they will escort you and make sure there

are no further problems on your journey," Big Tree said as he rose and hugged Crooked Nose.

"My friend I fear that as great as your victory was over Sheridan you still have a ways to go when it comes to being as great a warrior chief as Big Tree."

"Why do you say that?"

"Because only a student of war would lead his people into a box canyon with only one way out to be picked off like flies should they try to escape through the only exit."

Crooked Nose smiled.

"We are only here for a couple of hours before we move on."

"It only takes a minute for Sheridan or someone like him to pin you down here. I will leave enough men on the outside to assure your safety and in the morning I will send more to make sure that you are not disturbed for the remainder of your trip.

Tell me something Crooked Nose. Is it true that you travel with a band of niggras with a great war chief named Caesar."

"A great war chief and a friend…"

"Perhaps I will one day meet this great war chief."

"You are welcome to now."

"No. I fear my stay has been too long and I would hate to think of what my men are thinking and with you being in this box canyon I think it best I get back before I have to beg for more mercy for some stupidity my braves will commit," he said smiling.

The two men hugged again before parting ways.

August 9th

We crossed into Mexico this morning to the relief of everyone accept Crooked

Nose who sent his braves out to summon the Arapahos, the Biloxi, Southern Cheyenne as

well as Comanches and Apaches. I'm sure he invited more but that is all I can recall at

this time. He also called for the Mexican authorities to document that we had come in

peace and would not be encroaching on anyone's tribal lands and were only here because

the United States federal government had breached another treatise and called for their

removal and extermination. This was the first order of business and was done out of

respect to the neighboring tribes.

In a month or so I saw how much power my friend Crooked Nose really commanded as thousands of Indians from all over the western part of the United States arrived. Indian dignitaries from all over ascended upon Free Town to discuss the upheaval and removal of the Indian from the western hemisphere. From as far away as the Black Hills of the Dakotas came the mighty Sioux led by Sitting Bull and from California there came Chief Joseph of the Nez Perce.

Most of my people had never encountered a gathering of such enormity with so much pomp and ceremony and I must admit I too was taken back even though I was included.

Following the introductions it was firmly and quickly established that we all were suffering the same indignities from the same foe and that adversary of the red and Black man emanated from the United States government.

Each testimony reverberated the same story whether it came from Sitting Bull of the Sioux or Crooked Nose's testimony surrounding the Sand Creek Massacre the story was always the same. And in the end the question they ultimately arose was what we should do in response to the steady encroachment by the U.S. government?

During the second week of talks I found myself sitting to the side with mama and Aunt Petunia listening to the ongoing rhetoric.

"Ain't no need for all this here talk. If you ask me it's simple. You either fight or you leave. And being that they all in basically the same situation and in the jaws of the lion it seems to me that it's a pretty easy decision. Ain't a one of them tribes winning against the United States government. They way too big and too strong. What they better do is pack up and come down here where there's a government welcoming them. I don't see the sense of all that posturin' when the writing's on the wall."

Moments later Monica joined us and I was surprised when mama and auntie welcomed her as if she'd been family all along.

"All of this talk. What's it been? A week now? And what have they come up with? Seems a bit overdramatic if you ask me. They don't have an option."

Mama and Aunt Petunia both turned to Monica.

"She sounds just like him don't she," mama said laughing.

"If you ask me she sounds exactly like you," Aunt Petunia laughed.

"Hush. I'm trying to hear. That Roman Nose is one god lookn' red devil," mama said smiling.

I was definitely missing something. Both mama and Aunt Petunia who were very particular about who they allowed in their inner circle seemed to have already embraced Monica as if she were some long lost cousin and I still didn't have a clue who she was or what the connection was.

A few days later the camp was broken up and the talks ended. When it was all over I still didn't know what had been accomplished. All I got from the week long talks was that a group of very proud men had gotten together though not to arrange an alliance but to share the atrocities that had befallen them and to inspire and hearten their brethren in a losing battle of resistance

Meanwhile we moved a few days south as there was continued talk of Texas being annexed and we did not want to fall under U.S. rule again.

The land though not as good as the plains we'd left was good and the weather warmer seasonally.

After three months and most of our homes completed aside from some odds and ends we seem to have finally found our home. Crooked Nose taking the lead from us has settled in less than a quarter mile from us with many of his people interspersed with ours

and ours with his. It is something to behold and the spring should bring a host of new mothers.

And with Mandy along with Man in jail for the murder of Buck I am once again alone. Mama splits the care of my son with Monica and Aunt Petunia and I fear he is going to have a shoot first talk later attitude but they will not let me near him so overprotective are they as if they're grooming him to be the next great ruler of this earthly empire we call Free Town.

All in all, I like the way we have settled into our little town and we look to be moving in the right direction. Next week we hold our first election for city council sheriff and mayor of Free Town.

So far we have established four schools and are in the process of building more. Between mama, Celeste and Aunt Petunia pushing that they be the first to be built along with a hospital there was little for me to say.

I saw little of Crooked Nose during this time but with Yellow Knife as my neighbor I knew he was kept abreast of my actions. The majority of my time now was with the ranch and my growing herd. I had over three hundred now and the herd was growing quickly. Yellow Knife owned a herd of close to two hundred and between the

sale and trade with Texas settlers and the Mexican government it soon came to be so profitable that we started buying Texas Longhorns and began breeding them as well.

The remainder of my time I spent with the troops making sure they trained right and were in shape but most of all I set things in motion to keep them on their toes and competitive. I set up regular events with Crooked Nose where we would compete against his braves to stay sharp on our military skills. These were lively events which both sides took pride in. It was also a time of great betting where a win could make you comfortable for life.

We had little or no contact with outsiders during this time but we all agreed that the first order of business should be our safety and in the end and after a town hall

meeting that lasted close to four hours it was decided to build a fort large enough to defend ourselves against a Comanche raid or any other intruders. I took the proposal to Cooked Nose who gave his support and a legion of men to help with the construction and work was soon underway.

Monica who lived a quarter of a mile down the road from me and was my closest neighbor had and made herself a part of my daily life usually sharing dinner with me after which we would sit on the front porch 'til we were both half asleep at which time I would

take her home in my buckboard. Sometimes we would wake up in the wee hours of the morning and meet to go fishing together. She always said that the fish bite better at four in the morning but from what we caught I do believe that they too were sleep. On other days we would go hunting and snare a rabbit or kill a deer. And although I hate to admit it she was much better shooter. She'd skin it and make venison stew that was almost as good as mama's. At other times I'd sit and watch as she bathed naked down at the creek. When I first saw her in his fashion I was amazed at her beauty. I stood there while she proceeded to leave the stream and greet me. I must have appeared a fool as I stared unable to speak as she stood before me naked as a jaybird. My need for her had grown exponentially but there was little I could do. Each time I approached the subject she would simply say 'soon' and I was sorry I'd ever uttered those words.

What Monica had accomplished in the short time I'd known her was to become my friend, my partner, my soul mate and it felt good. I had never had a friend to whom I could speak freely without being conscious of their interest. But she who wanted nothing more than to converse and enjoy life made life simpler and helped me put today's needs on the backburner.

She's the type of woman you take as a wife.

August 7th

Well it is three o'clock and the general election is over. It looks like Aunt Petunia is mayor. How that happened I will never know unless it possibly has something to do with mama being her campaign manager and no one wanting to oppose mama. It was a good strategy although I wouldn't consider that a fair election. Mama is I charge of the city council and we have a new sheriff. I was voted as commander and cf of the council which includes the army so I guess little has changed.

Celeste is in charge of the schools while Monica was somehow placed in charge of the library. I am still trying to understand how this young woman has risen so in just a few short months. With mama and auntie still in charge it's almost as if they have known

her for some time and she is somehow part of the Free Town aristocracy. It is obvious they must know something of her being sent North to Oberlin College to select her to head the library. But how do they know her and why have they chosen to put their faith in her. It has continued to bother and I don't know why I have waited so long to ask mama. I will do so the first thing tomorrow.

August 8th

I awoke to the sounds of gunfire this morning and every able bodied man rushing to the Northern border of Free Town. The walled side of the fort was holding well and the scant, few men on duty had no problem holding off the attacking Indians.

"I'm thinking these walls were a good investment," Yellow Knife said smiling.

"But why are they attacking us?" I said laying my sights on an Indian rushing to the wall on foot.

"They are Apaches. That is what they do," Yellow Knife laughed. "But it looks like you have things well in hand so I am going back to the ranchero. I have two fillies about to foal. If you run into any problems send a runner and I will send you some braves back,"

When the Indians saw their numbers begin to dwindle they began to retreat at which time I went to see how we had fared. Approaching Boston who was now my second in command I asked how we'd done.

"Like a turkey shoot boss. Just like a turkey shoot," he said grinning the way only Boston can do.

"Well, just keep your eyes open. They may circle back."

The rest of the day was quiet but the evening brought with it more calamity when out of the blue Celeste rode up to the house. I was sitting there talking to Monica as we did every night after dinner.

"Caesar, Monica. How are you both this beautiful summer evening?"

"Good. Good Celeste. Just out for a ride tonight?"

"Yes. You know I've been so busy just trying to get everything up and running so these kids can start school that I haven't taken time to come up for air. So, tonight I thought I'd just get away and breathe deeply. I just needed some time for me."

"I think we all do. These last six months haven't been easy for any involved." Monica replied.

"And somehow we all made it through unscathed," I added.

"Yes, thanks to you and the good Lord above," Monica added.

"Were you ever afraid Caesar?"

"Every minute of every hour of everyday."

"But you led us through and now we're in a land where we can breathe and be free to be human."

"Through his blessings we have been put in the Promised Land. I was just His shepherd leading His flock. But what makes me most happy is that the people have garnered the spirit to grow and prosper independently of a governing force telling them how to proceed with their lives. It was Monica who suggested setting up the city council.

And it's funny but I go to the city council meetings from time-to-time and can't help laughing. They can't agree on anything and it takes them awhile to come to any decision."

"But they do make a decision unlike you Caesar. Ever since I've known you were always caught between one thing or another. Seems easy enough to lead thousands of people but oh so difficult for you to make choices in your own life," Celeste countered before mounting up. "'Nite Monica."

"G'nite Celeste," Monica said smiling before turning to look at Caesar who sat there stunned.

"What just happened?"

"I do believe your friend Celeste is overheating and tired of waiting on you. But anyway she said she wants you and wants to know what's taking you so long to make a commitment. That's what it boils down to coupled with the fact that she feels threatened

by our relationship and is a tad bit jealous. I'll tell you though she's expecting you to come by tonight and make amends. She'll give you the world tonight and make you a very happy man in turn for your commitment. You'd better go get a taste of that hot apple pie. "

"Cherry has always been my favorite. I think I'll have to pass and just continue to be patient until my slice comes around."

"You sure that's going to happen?" Monica laughed.

"Soon?" I said.

"Soon," Monica repeated before leaning and kissing me hard and passionately. It was the first time we'd touched lips and I could remember seeing fireworks when I was just a kid and for the first time since then there were explosions. I tell you it was a glorious thing and I never knew two people could make each other feel this way.

"Monica."

"Stop Caesar. Sleep on it. I don't want you to blurt anything out because you're feeling some sort of way of way right through here. We're young. We have plenty of time to make some of life's rougher choices. Really there's no rush. Let's just try and build the types of lives both of us want and then we can see where we're at and how good

a friends we've become then perhaps we can reassess how we really feel about each other. I guess what I'm trying to say Caesar is let's take our time. Come and get to know me."

"I am trying in case you haven't noticed."

"Oh, I've noticed and you're doing very well. Right now I think you have more pressing concerns. There's a very pretty lady in need of your company."

"And I'm in need of hers. What do you suggest we do this evening?"

"You know what I'm talking about Caesar. You'd better get over to Celeste's before you lose her completely."

"I do believe I made my choice long before tonight Monica."

"Okay but you really should say something to her. She rode all the way out here to get you to understand that she wants you. To ignore her would crush her and show utter disregard for her feelings and your friendship."

"Sometimes life is hard. I held an olive branch for her for over a year and she never responded. Sometime the worst thing in life is missed opportunity." And I knew his decision was final.

Leaning over and resting her head on his lap Monica closed her eyes to the world.

August 12th

The days have been so cluttered I haven't had a chance to write. Mama came by to check on me and the baby while making her rounds and checking on the status of her the residents. She's taken the office of the first mayor of Free Town very seriously and is constantly in contact with the residents and intent on making improvements where needed. I think much of her motivation comes from the fact that since papa's gone there's a void in her life. Aunt Petunia is no different seemingly content to muddle around her little garden humming to herself? Mama said to leave her alone. Said Aunt Petunia's strong but I still worry about her and keep an eye on her. She seems to lost that zest for

life that kept her bubbly and smiling. I'm pretty sure that that thing she lost, that zest that made waking up every day a joy is Uncle Andrew and she is still grieving deeply. Sometimes when a mate completes you and they die unexpectedly and too soon and it's always too soon the surviving spouse seems to die along with them. I think that's what's happening to auntie. She seems lost without Uncle Andrew in her life.

There is no other news to write. There is only work. I will write again when there is something of circumstance.

September 15th

The Lord is a good God! He watches out over me and mine. I awoke this morning to the sound of a trumpet sounding and I immediately gabbed my guns and went to the north wall to see what all the fuss was about.

A little boy of about eight or nine who seemed to have taken up the job as company crier must have noticed my bewilderment and shouted.

"Soldiers approaching! Soldiers approaching!"

I pushed the filly along at a gallop now. I knew the wall with snipers atop it was virtually impregnable but I was still curious to know where our latest threat arose from. Boston, Yellow Knife and Monica were already there. Mama had basically given up her command by this time so busy was she with being mayor. Michael, Joshua's oldest son had taken over her command but I did not see him ad assumed he was with his unit.

"What is it?"

"There is a small army of men just out of eyesight. They don't seem to be posing a threat. They seem to set up some sort of camp there. They've been there for the last hour or so. They seem to just be milling around," Boston noted.

"Let me see the binoculars."

"I could barely make out anything more than the outline of men who seemed like Boston said to be just milling around.

"Do I have any volunteers to ride with me under a white flag of truce to see what it is these men want."

Yellow Knife and Boston mounted their horses and were ready within minutes.

"Give me a chance to get into position with the snipers to cover you. Let it be known when you speak to these men that any sudden movements and we will cut them down like ribbons," Monica whispered to me. I nodded in agreement and waited til she

and our best six snipers moved out and flanked the camp before we trotted out. I had done this before. And each time I did I was more than just a little afraid and now was no different. At fifty yards or so we stopped to see if they had their sights set on us but the camp did not seem the least bit aroused by our presence and the men kept on doing whatever it was that they were doing.

At that point we got down off our mounts and walked into the campsite. An eerie feeling came over me at this time. And for some reason I didn't feel like I was in a strange campsite but almost as if I were home. These men. These men I knew. And then there in the distance I saw father and Uncle Andrew. It had to be a dream. Was I dreaming. Seeing them I ran and hugged each both together and apart. Here were my father ad my uncle in one piece. These men who are feared dead now stood before me strong and as proud as I'd ever seen them.

"Uncle Andrew, papa we made it. We made it."

The men laughed and then papa spoke.

"There was never any doubt that you wouldn't. You come from prime stock," the two men laughed.

"Mother will be so happy to see you? And I fair Aunt Petunia is fading away right before our eyes she grieves you so. Let me go and tell them the news. Come. Leave your things. I will send some men for them later."

"No. son we have travelled a long way. Bring our wives to us. I don't think we are quite up for a parade yet," Papa laughed.

Just then Monica and her men walked into camp.

"Monica. I am so glad to see you made it," papa said hugging her as if he had known her all his life.

"Monica. I am glad to see you kept a close eye on young Caesar. He seems to look fairly fit. I know you were of invaluable service to him and I want to thank you." Uncle Andrew added.

I was shocked. So, Monica had been in their employ the entire time but how? Why?

I'd had enough.

"Papa, Uncle Andrew what's this about? Did you send Monica to look after me?"

"Why no we didn't son. It was Uncle Ben who insisted on her looking after your well-being."

"Uncle Ben saw you as the heir apparent and the future fo us as a people and figured there would be some resentment and some jealousy once you got settled and insisted on sending his granddaughter to look after you."

"His granddaughter?"

"Yes. You don't remember when you two used to play when you were just toddlers?"

No. I didn't remember her. I had never seen her before in my life but that answered a lot of questions like why she seemed so close to our family. Uncle Ben was family.

"When it looked bleakest Uncle Ben sent Monica with a contingent of about ten or so more to safety since it looked liked doomsday at the point. Monica had arrived home from Boston right during our toughest times and Lord knows she was a boon to us. In all honesty I have yet to see a better shot. There were times that she kept those

crackers at bay with just a single repeating carbine. Just her by her lonesome... So, Ben thought it would be a waste to lose her. And he sent her out here to look after you. How did she do?"

"She saved my life on more than one occasion either by her marksmanship or her guile. She makes my days easier."

"Sounds though she has taken care of you to the extent there may be some feelings there than you are letting onto?"

"I don't doubt that there are," I said grabbing Monica and pulling her tightly to me.

"Where is Uncle Ben?" I was so full of questions that I didn't know where to start.

Uncle Andrew looked at Monica and then at papa.

"Uncle Ben didn't make it. He made it through the fighting but when there was nothing left and we were forced to leave he died. I think more than anything else it was the fact that he was forced off of his land that he had labored so hard for. I think it killed him. I'm sorry Monica."

"Grandpa lived a full life," she said as the tears rolled down her face."He raised me by himself and taught me everything I know."

Now I knew! Monica had been the little tomboy who used to follow Uncle Ben everywhere. If Uncle Ben went fishing and took us with him she was always there. When he took us hunting she was always there. We were kids then and we used to always wonder why this kid got to hang around Uncle Ben all the time. Sometimes we would be out just wandering through the woods and there was Uncle Ben teaching her to shoot or shoot a bow and arrow. We thought she was the luckiest kid in the world to have someone like Uncle Ben take you under his wing and teach you everything there was to know about the world.

So, this was Monica. Riding back in the gates of Free Town side-by-side with Monica I tried to get her mind off her grandfather's death with some idle conversation. I almost felt bad for feeling so good about having my father and uncle back in my life.

Lord knows my God is a good God. Ad here was my favorite person in the world grieving for just having lost the closest and only family she'd ever known.

"So, why didn't you just tell me Uncle Ben had sent you?"

"Because not recognizing me why would you accept a complete stranger to be your guardian angel? Besides it really had nothing to do with you Caesar. It could have been anyone. Grandfather had a job he wanted done and thought I was the best person to

carry it out and that's what I did. You may not know what you are worth to our community and maybe to Blacks folks as a whole in the future but others see your worth and feel it would be in the interest of all to keep you safe from yourself and others until you realize that you have been destined for greatness. And I for one have been one to see it if you could just manage to stay out of your own way," she said before galloping off.

I wasn't sure if she was upset with me or just upset over her grandfather's passing. But now I wanted to see mama's face when she saw papa had returned.

When papa entered mama's home I thought she'd had a hard attack falling out right then and there. Papa only laughed.

"She'll be alright son. I think the shock of it all was a bit too much for her. I'll take care of her. You go home and get some rest so you can bring me up-to-date tomorrow."

I nodded and hugged him again so glad was I to see him.

I only wish I could have been there to see the reunion between auntie and Uncle Andrew. On the way home, I rode past Monica's house. Sitting on the porch in a long black gown I rode up.

"Mind if I sit for a spell," I asked.

When she didn't answer I walked up the porch steps and had a seat beside her on the swing. Usually so clear focused and upbeat she was quiet and withdrawn. I knew she was grieving and so I just sat and held her in my arms until she went to sleep before taking her in and putting her to bed and locking up.

Setember 17th

Spent much of the morning with the family listening to papa and Uncle Andrew's tales of being locked up for leading the battles at Three Winds. And how it was Sheriff Fernhill had secured their escape. They'd then gone from there to Washington to plead their case and

receive compensation for lands that had been confiscated from them. The reception had been good and now Uncle Andrew was only awaiting restitution.

"Your uncle is going to be one of the richest niggra you or I have ever had the occasion to know, "Aunt Petunia said with pride but more than that it was because with her Andrew back in the fold she was whole again.

Mama seemed to shadow papa and I felt for him. I know she'd kept him up half the night telling him of every second of our trip. And now she was going to take them to see Crooked Nose.

It was good to have papa and Uncle Andrew back in the fold again but if we were to survive the winter and be ready for the upcoming spring I needed to be working. So, much as I wanted to see Crooked Nose's reactions when he met papa and Uncle Andrew I had to decline.

By this time, Yellow and I had become partners and combined our herds. We now had over a thousand and nearly that in cattle and business was good. Between selling to the Mexican government, the Indians and the settlers we couldn't have asked for more and there was constant traffic. Now we were in the process of clearing a little over a hundred acres. In the spring we would try our hand at cotton and tobacco.

Monica estimated after looking over the books that we were making somewhere in the neighborhood of three to four thousand a month. More than comfortable I still had close to a hundred thousand from the bank heists we had pulled off in and around Jackson and was considering opening a general store and running a supply wagon train from points east to a

trading post in Indian territory. We could man it with troops and have them ride shotgun with the supply train. They would be moonlighting when not on duty and could put a few

dollars in their pockets. Monica worked out the details figuring the cost of such a venture and when she'd finished and we'd reviewed it for what seemed the thousandth time finding no fault and how great the profit margin we set about at once to set it up.

It was Monica who would ride the route procuring agents, trading posts and general stores as potential customers. We both agreed that she being an intelligent and attractive woman she'd be the best possible candidate for garnering customers and I agreed that she could go and speak on behalf of me if she'd do things. For one she had to agree equal partners in this latest venture. And last but not least she had to agree to marry me.

Now the first she had no problem with but the whole marriage thing seemed to throw

her for a loop as she said she really needed time to think on it and would let me know when

she returned.

September 18th

Monica pulled out this morning accompanied by twenty five men I considered my best soldiers. Last night I asked this woman to marry me and Lord knows I don't want anything to happen to her before she has a chance to answer. Seems now the tables have turned. Now I am paying for her safety.

I went to visit my friend Crooked Nose today. I guess I've been so preoccupied with the ranch and businesses I've neglected my friendship.

"Well, well... My friend finally comes to visit me."

"Yes. Although I heard you might be taking on a new wife and I didn't want to intrude."

"You do not lie well my friend. But how are you> Yellow Knife keeps me informed of most things but he like you is so caught up in the running of your ranch that he does not stop to smoke with an old man either."

"I think everyone's just preparing for the winter so they don't get caught with their pants down."

"And speaking of which I would like for you to sell me a few hundred head of cattle. I think it is time for me to go into the ranching business. I can sell a few and used the rest to feed the people over the winter months."

"No problem Crooked Nose. I will send over two hundred head and we will discuss the price later."

"Make it a fair price."

"Have I ever done you wrong my friend?"

"No. I can't say you have but men have a way of going from friends to enemies where money is concerned."

"There is no amount of money that is greater than your friendship to me Crooked Nose."

"And let there never be," he said standing and hugging me.

Crooked Nose's oldest daughter entered the teepee and had a seat.

"Yes daughter is there something that you which to speak to me about?"

"No father. Actually it is Caesar that I wish to speak to,"

"Speak Sonya," Crooked Nose said somewhat disturbed that we had been interrupted.

"What I wanted to speak to Caesar about is private father. I just stopped in so he wouldn't leave without me having a chance to speak to him."

"I see. Well, we are almost finished here. He will be out shortly," Crooked Nose said.

All I had done was try to get away from my thoughts and the thought that Monica was gone and would be gone the better part of a month perhaps even longer. It had been my hopes that perhaps my friend would join me and go fishing and wile away the day. Now this. I couldn't possibly see what Sonya wold have to talk about. Careful not to insult Crooked Nose I had made it more than clear to his daughter that I did not want to be bothered. So why this?

It was difficult now trying to hold a conversation with my friend who was quite curious in the way I was leading the people.

"You know I can remember when I was a boy and we had a grand old cabin back in South Carolina. My father had even bought into owning slaves and raising tobacco. He was quite adept at it as well until the government decided they could get rich by selling our land. Our people farmed then. We raise squash, beans, watermelons—you name it—and we raised it. We grew tobacco and cotton and exported it and did well. When we were forced to move west into Indian Territory we let it go and began to hunt buffalo so I am surprised at how easily the people took to getting back to the soil. I like it though. My young braves are trading their horses for seed and are already boasting of who will have the largest crop."

"What will be your cash crop?"

"I tell them to concentrate on cotton, sugar and tobacco depending on what this land will support."

"I think we have chosen a good fertile piece of land that will support all three. I think you have made a wise choice my friend. Now let me go and see what this beautiful young lady wants from this battle weary old soldier."

"You are neither battle wearied or old. I would trade your youth and exuberance for what is ahead of me any sunrise."

Rising I hugged my old friend and promised t see him before the week was out.

Exiting his teepee I found Sonya playing entertaining four little Indian girls and I stood amazed as the girls followed her lead in a sing-a-long that revealed the most beautiful voice. She did not stop when she saw me and finished with girls by hugging them all before they ran off in search of some more merriment.

"I'm sorry to disturb your meeting with father." Her English was perfect and I

wondered why she had never chosen to me before now.

"You know I can't think of another man he holds in such regard."

"That is good to know but before you go any further make I make a request?"

"Why certainly. I was hoping not to have to be this forward but you are the only man

I know that has not made a request of me," she said suddenly smiling.

"Sonya have you given any thought to teaching? It has been brought to my attention

that the way to success for our young people is through education."

It was obviously not the question she was expecting to hear and I could see her

demeanor change.

"Let's walk. I have a favorite place that I sometimes go when I want to be alone to

think. Sonya led me up a steep ravine through thicket until we came to a bluff high above

Free Town. The view was amazing and we sat there staring for several minutes before

speaking.

"Caesar I am fast approaching thirty and I am afraid that father is wondering if I am

to ever take a husband. Sometimes I wonder myself. But the braves who chase me do not

interest me. I see bigger things for me and my people. What you have done is to lead us into

the modern world. The way of the Cheyenne is gone as we know it but there is a future. You

have seen it and my people are slowly beginning to embrace it although many of the older

members of our tribe will never accept the white man's ways. I think father sees it to. My

dream is to be with a man that also shares my vision and from what I can see that man is you.

Our union would bring our people together and we could lead both our people with

the same vision."

All she had said was true but what she didn't understand was that despite her beauty and simple elegance I had already committed myself to Monica who gave me everything I could possibly want and need.

"Yellow Knife has already told me that there is a woman in your life that you spend a considerable amount of time with and although I don't know this woman I am sure that she is some woman to have made you notice her. I am not trying to steal you away but only ask that you give me time so I can show you what I have to bring to the table Caesar. Take your time in deciding but give me the opportunity to entertain you."

"I am truly flattered. And the woman you speak of has gone east for some time to conduct business on our behalf. I don't suppose she will object for me having made a new friend," I said lying to both her and me.

The smile returned to Sonya's face.

"Then my wish has come true," she said grinning from ear-to-ear.

"Tell me this then Sonya. You mean to tell me that with over five thousand young braves you cannot find one that interests you?"

"I never said that none interest me. I said I did not like the way the Cheyenne have not moved into modern society."

"I'm sorry. I'm not following you."

"When I was young and they started moving people from our homeland in the east my father sent me away to a northern Jesuit school for Indians. There I learned to read and write. And there I read of love and there my conception of love was born. I guess in a way I became Americanized. That is not to say that I lost my way or my Cheyenne traditions

but this idea of one brave taking on many wives does not appeal to me and I do not want to be held like a piece of property to be called upon when the whim hits my husband and that is why I am not interested in any of my father's braves."

"I think I understand but then why do you not tell your father how you feel?"

"Tell my father. Why would a man with three wives understand? But your people do not believe in such. And I have found a wonderful, beautiful young man that I do not fear sharing my teepee with during those cold, long winter nights." she said smiling before letting her deerskin dress hit the ground.

I could feel myself breaking out in sweat. It has been close to a year now since I'd slept with the mother of my child and both Celeste and Monica had rejected my overtures. And now standing before naked was an Indian princess like none I'd ever known before. Her body tight and erect she stood before me her nipples hard pointing at me accusingly.

Clearly shook by these turn of events I stood and embraced her before bending over and picking up her dress and handing it to her. Smiling dejectedly she took it from me.

Walking back to my horse she grabbed my hand.

"The worst thing a man can do to a woman is to reject her when she offers herself to you. But let it be known Caesar Augustus. I will have you. Trust me. Woman or no woman I will have you."

To tell you the truth I was flattered if not a little afraid. I'd promised Crooked Nose I would see him before the week was out. Now I was not so sure.

September 19th

Since father and Uncle Andrew have returned I have seen little of them. From what I hear tell mama and Aunt Petunia have kept them pretty well occupied showing them what needs to be done to improve Free Town but these are not the same men that we left when we left Three Winds. They seem happy enough to laze around down by the creek when they are not under their wives careful watch. Uncle Andrew even stopped by and seemed pleasantly surprised by the size of the herd and the fine breeding we had induced but that was it and later on that day when I went to see if he had any suggestions I found him and papa and a jug of hooch down by the creek laughing and fishing

I returned to the ranch and found most of the hands heading home or milling around the bunk house. This was usually I spent with Monica and I missed her already. I decided to call it an early night and wondered how Monica was faring so far when sleep overtook me. I was awakened not long after when I heard what appeared to be a lone rider. Getting up and

going to the window I neither saw a horse or rider and was returning to bed when I saw a

shadow in the doorway. Racing to the large armoire where I kept several of my pistols a

voice surrounded me.

"I told you I would have you Caesar. Now lie down."

Two young braves one of which brandished a long saber stood to her right while an

older brave carrying a Springfield rifle aimed at my head stood to her left. Taking the rifle

and keeping it trained on me she shouted at the braves.

"Strip him and tie him down to the bed."

When I looked to fight them off she fired a warning shot that narrowly missed me

and I was thencompliant. Once stripped and tied to the bed posts with long strips of rawhide

she turned to her accomplices and dismissed them.

"You can leave us now. I don't believe Mr. Augustus will be causing any more problems."

The two men left and Sonya pulled a chair up bedside.

"Caesar, why do you have to make things so difficult? Can you not see that I am in love with you? I mean to have you one way or another. You will have sex with me and after awhile you will come to love me but right now it is I that needs to feel you inside of me. And you will be gentle and make it fine since this is my very first time. I will make it good for you and you will ask the next time if you can make love to me. That is how good I will make you feel."

And Sonya was right about that taking everything I had to give and making me want for more. I was sore and spent when she untied me and smiled before kissing me passionately and walking out the door.

I had both trouble standing and walking that day and found myself in a daze as though I had when Buck and I had drunk that bad hooch but I hadn't had anything to drink and then I thought of Sonya going to get me some water when she'd taken a break and I wondered if she had put something in the water. After drinking it I remember little other than her smacking me in attempts to revive before making me watch as she took me again."

Not sure of what to do I sought out Uncle Andrew and told him of Sonya.

"Women can be dangerous and I think this one is more dangerous than most. What she is messing with is the peace between two people s and your friendship with Crooked Nose. He asked you to entertain her with the hopes that you two would form a union or an alliance between our peoples which would serve our people well. I know you don't love this girl but the sacrifice you may have to make will before the good of the thousands not your own."

"So what you're telling me is to marry her for the good of the people and in spite of the fact that I feel nothing for her?"

"What are your options Caesar? If she goes to her father around this he will believe his daughter and in his mind you will have defiled her and she will always be torn even if he finds reason to forgive you. There will always be that doubt in his mind. Things will never be as they were. And that me m nephew is the best case scenario. You do not want to consider the worst."

"My God uncle can it get any worse? When things just begin to finally fall into place and seem so right."

"She could turn out to be just the one for you," he chuckled. "Don't know if you noticed but she's a very pretty girl," he said walking to his horse.

"So, what you're telling me is that I have no other alternative?"

"You might try running. Other than that I'd start practicing your 'yes dears," he said

laughing as he walked away.

"This is not funny uncle."

"I wouldn't think it would be from your standpoint but from mine it's hilarious.

What I wouldn't give to be a fly on the wall to see how you break the news to Monica when

she returns," he said doubling over in laughter now. "And by the way, how's Celeste doing?

You know son there are worse things in life than having three beautiful women wanting

you."

I thought about what Uncle Andrew said and I readily accepted the fact that I was

leading a blessed life up until this point. And many a man would be tickled about the

situation I now found myself in but I'd finally found some peace and contentment. I was

most happy in the company of Monica whether we were competing against each other or just

sitting on the front porch in each other's company. I's finally met my equal and my soul

mate Now this.

Up until now the truth had always worked for me. Often times it came at a severe cost to those involved but I believed in confronting issues with the truth and to let the chips fall where they may. Uncle Andrew may have found humor in my dilemma but I saw little humor and would see Yellow Knife and ask for his opinion. But after explaining the situation to Yellow Knife and giving him Uncle Andrew's whole take on the situation Yellow Knife had a seat on the corral fence and did not say anything for a long while.

"I have to agree with everything you uncle tells you my friend. That is the road with the least amount of obstacles. That is what she wants. And she is very beautiful. She is loyal and will devote her life to you. Many of my braves would die to be in your place. It is the logical choice as well and would do wonders in bringing the Cheyenne nation and your people together. The possibilities are endless if you consummate this union Caesar."

"I know the benefits of marrying Sonya Yellow Knife and how it would strengthen our alliance with your people but do you not understand that every action that I commit I have been groomed for. I was given the responsibility of leading my people here and settling a land I knew nothing of. I was responsible for the safety of lives of my people. And now that I have accomplished that feat and lifted the weight off my shoulders I am told that I have to marry this woman for the sake our people. I understand the implications for all except me. When am I allowed to live my life? When do the responsibilities of the people become their responsibility?"

"With leadership come great responsibilities. Do not worry about Monica. She will understand but what I suggest you do my friend is grab the bull by the horns and man up. You do not know Cheyenne women. If you allow her Sonya will run roughshod over you. She is a spoiled princess. Walk in and lay down the law. Do not allow her one concession?

You never know? She may change her mind. She has never had anyone dictate to her or put expectations on her. Treat her as you do Monica and expect her to work and do on your behalf. Make her see that the more you prosper in realizing your dreams the more she will prosper in her own. I'm telling you to be demanding and make her pull her own weight. If she cannot or does not see fit to then she will return to her father's house. If she does however meet your expectations then you will have a wonderful marriage. My marriage too was arranged and though it was difficult in the beginning I have come to cherish Few Moons."

"So, you think I should marry Sonya even though I am not in love with her?"

"I do not think my friend. I know this is something that you must do."

I took both Yellow Knife's and Uncle Andrew's advice under careful consideration and knew that both men had been in similar circumstances over the years and had been forced to make sacrifices. I suppose it just came with the territory.

They tell me that at one time Uncle Andrew was not even permitted to talk to Aunt Petunia by the master's wife because she too was in love with Uncle Andrew. And so for the good of the community he entertained this white woman and her demented desires until a time when he had wrestled control of Three Winds from her grasp. What a sacrifice that must have been.

In the following week, I grappled with my decision knowing full well that if this is what this Indian princess was calling for then chances were she would get her wish. I had

always said that women were smarter, wiser and more scandalous than men were and here

was just another case to prove my point. And to think Monica was coming back with an

answer to my marriage proposal.

September 28th

I have not felt like writing. Mama says I am depressed. I'm sure by now they all

know of my troubles but no one has volunteered any solutions other than Uncle Andrew

which means they are in concurrence with him that I should marry Sonya.

The only thing that seems to soothe me is my herd. When I am out there working

with them I hardly have a care in the world. And so I work with the horses from sunup to

sunset. And today is no different.

In bed by eight o'clock there seems little good in the days now.

I am awakened later that night by the sound of horses. As far as I can make out there

are four. I quickly reach for my rifle but before I can cock it and make it to the window I feel

someone behind me.

"Put your hands up and drop the rifle."

"Someone is at the door that wishes to see you."

I walked down the stairs ad opened the front door.

"Lovely night wouldn't you agree my pet?" Sonya said sitting sideways on the pretty brown sorrel. Two braves moved to her and helped her down.

"Come sit," she said patting the porch swing next to where she now sat. Her braves climbed back on their horses waiting on her next command.

"I haven't seen you since you were last here. I really thought the love I showed you would have brought you to me but I guess I was wrong. So, I thought I'd bring you back. Perhaps the second dosage will have a better affect. My only question is will my braves have to tie you down or will you give yourself to me voluntarily?"

It was then that I thought about Yellow Knife's remarks.

"You are attracted to me because like you father I am a leader of men ad possess many of the same characteristics that he does but we are men of principle and until I come to love you you will have to force me to make love to you."

'Then let it be so." Sonya nodded and the three braves were upon Caesar quickly.

"There is no need for that," Caesar said before getting up and leading the men upstairs to his bedroom where he disrobed and lay on his bed waiting for the men to tie him down. Once this was done Sonya dismissed the braves and pulled the chair to the bed where she sat staring for quite some time before speaking.

"I am deeply saddened by these turn of events Caesar. You have to excuse me for using this approach. Those are my father's braves but before that they are my friends. And so when I ask they comply. I am sure that most think what I do to you now but they are my

friends first so like I said they comply but they disagree with my tactics because I am the

daughter of Crooked Nose the great war chief of the Northern Cheyenne making me a

princess. They can hardly understand why a princess would or should have to go through

this when every Cheyenne brave would give their right arm to have the opportunity to be in

my company. No they do not understand but they are not the only ones.

The truth is I don't understand either. Why does the man I choose not want me? You

know they say I am beautiful. I do not see myself that way but they believe it and so I was

afforded everything and I admit I have grown used to that and have never been put in a

position where I have been pushed to the side and told no. You have done both and all I did

was fall in love from afar.

I could see if I wasn't capable of fulfilling your every need and assuring you the kind

of life a great leader is warranted if you would only open the door and allow me safe passage

to your heart.

Your rejection has hurt me deeply and I am afraid I have acted most despicably in

trying to gain your favor but there has to be a solution. I am sue that if you have spoken to

your mother and father they woud tell you a marriage to Sonya daughter of Crooked Nose

they would applaud the decision. Think of what it would mean to our people Caesar? Don't

be selfish man. It is no accident that your people and mine were fighting a war and we united

to ward off the enemy. That was no accident. Why can't you see? This is our destiny. We

can uplift our people. We can do this Caesar. You and I together can do great things. And

then there is you and I. I will make you so very happy all through the day and when you

blow the candles out at night. That said Sonya stood letting her buckskin dress fall to the

floor before straddling me. No words were spoken but I felt her this time. I felt her passion

and her anguish and I knew that all she had said was true. Now it was just a matter of me

coming to grips with the idea and breaking the news to Monica.

"The next time I come to see you you will take me in your arms and you will love me

the way a woman like me needs to be loved. And there will be no need for my father's

braves."

Not here would be no need for braves.

September 29th

"Saw riders last night, looked like braves," Yellow Knife commented.

"Couldn't tell whether they were wearing war paint though."

"I'm still not sure."

"Sonya and her braves?"

"Yeah."

"How did it go?"

"Told me the same thing everyone else has. It would be good for the people."

"And?"

"There is no 'and'."

"So, you're gonna marry her then?"

"Do I have a choice?."

"Why you lucky son of a gun... I'd trade Few Moons in right now if I had the opportunity. Congratulations my friend. Sonya is a very beautiful woman. The gods have smiled on you my friend. Have you told her yet?"

"There's not much in talking with Sonya. She's quite astute. She tells you and when it's over you find that she's right and there's little argument left. When she left she made the comment that on her next visit there would be no need for her father's braves. I took that to mean we are getting married and there is no need for you to continually oppose. That's what I took it to mean."

"Well, all I can say is that you are doing the best thing. When will you tell her?"

"After I speak to Monica."

"I think Monica will take it well. She is a good soldier and understands the grand scheme of things. She will do what's best in the interest for the community as a whole."

"I sure hope so. You know I asked her to marry me when she left. She said she'd let me know when she got back."

"Well, let's hope she turns you down."

"That would makes things a might easier but it still doesn't solve my issues with marrying a woman I hardly know and don't love."

"You make too big a deal out of love. When a woman looks as good as Sonya does you can learn to fall in love with her," Yellow Knife laughed. "But seriously my friend I have watched Sonya grow into the woman she has become and she is a very, sweet and caring woman. You will not find many better."

"It's hard to tell with a gun pointed at my head."

"She's just trying to make a point," Yellow Knife said smiling. "Cheyenne woman are not used to being told no."

Later that afternoon I found my way to Crooked Nose's camp and spoke with him for awhile but it was not Crooked Nose who I was in search of. I don't know what drew me to look for her but here I was.

"Oh Caesar what a pleasant surprise," she said grabbing my hand and pulling me along. "I hope this visit means you've given it some thought and finally come to realize that our marriage would best serve all the parties involved."

"This is not a summit or a sit down to draw up a deal for a peace treaty. This is a marriage. Everyone I've talked to looks at this marriage as being beneficial to our people. No one has yet to ask me how I feel about you as a woman as a wife."

"Well, then let be the first to ask you. What do you think of me as a woman?" she said before letting her clothes fall to the ground and turning so that I could take in all of her. "So, tell me what do you think of me as a woman?"

"Why do you feel it so necessary for me to tell you how beautiful you are when you already know?"

"It's important to me to know that my future husband thinks I'm beautiful on the outside and when he gets to know me he will find that my beauty on the outside only pales when compared to my beauty on the inside. But the inner beauty you will only be able to appreciate with time."

"Does it matter at all that I am already in love?"

"To some extent and I'm not sure that I know the extent of your love for this woman but I don't know if you remember me telling you last night that I am used to having

what I want. And although I am not one to demand things I will tell you this on the graves of my ancestors. You will tell her that you cannot marry her because you no longer love her or she will not meet with a pretty end. As you know I have braves at the ready so if you truly love this woman you will see that she is no longer a part of our lives or harm will befall her."

I looked at his woman lying next to me naked and there was no doubt in my mind that she would have Monica killed if no more than to make a point. Looking at her naked I soon grew hard and considered taking her right then and there if we hadn't heard horses in the distance.

Sonya threw her dress on quickly.

"It would not look good to be seen this far away from the village with you alone. But I will see you tonight. I will be alone. Leave the door open," she said before kissing me and dashing off through the woods on her way back to the village.

Boston and Yellow Knife rode up briskly.

"Comanches and Apaches attack with many braves. I think they are raiding for horses. They are fighting with my braves down on the southern tip but I don't feel as though we can hold them back much longer."

"And where are our troops," I shouted at Boston. "Free Town sir."

"And are they taking fire?"

"No sir."

"Then send half of them to help Yellow Knife's braves. Bring out the Gatling and see if we can't even the odds until we get better organized. Have they been out to breach the wall?"

"No Caesar but they are close enough and doing their best to set fire to it."

"And that's why we need the big guns. To keep them at bay… What are you waiting for man? Those guns aren't going to find themselves down here by themselves and get word to papa and my uncle to meet me."

"Yes sir," Boston said wheeling the big bay around and riding off.

"And what finds you here. You know we had a time finding you," Yellow Knife said smiling broadly knowing full well why I was there.

"Needed to try and explain things to Sonya."

"Did it do any good?"

"Don't really think so… She said she'd be stopping by the house tonight without her braves. So, what do you thnk?"

"I'd give both my arms and legs to live just one day of your life my friend," Yellow Knife laughed before riding off in the direction of the gunfire.

"Be careful of what you wish for my friend. Things are not always what they seem."

When I arrived it was hard to tell just how many Comanches and Apaches were attacking in the midst of all the smoke and chaos but I knew after a few minutes that this was a larger war party than I had imagined and they were relentless; making several well-planned charges at the southern gates. Yellow Knifes braves fought with a great deal of ferocity and passion but were so outnumbered hat I feared they would be overrun at any minute.

It was then that Boston and one or two units of our finest artillery units arrived attaching the Gatlings to the wall. After a few well aimed bursts from the big guns the charges slowed to a minimum and in little less than thirty minutes late we heard no return

fire. Yellow Knife and Crooked Nose called it a resounding victory although by this time

Crooked Nose was so sure that I would handle it that he didn't bother leaving his lodge.

Come to think of it neither had papa or Uncle Andrew and if I knew them they were sitting

down by the creek fishing.

Later that evening Yellow Knife and I sat down by the corral watching the horses

when a rider rode up. To no one's surprise it was Sonya dressed in an all-white deerskin

dress with matching moccasins and a turquoise necklace and ankle bracelet.

"You look like the princess you are. If I were to write a story book you would be my

choice for the beautiful princess. I was just telling Caesar how fortunate he was to have

someone so beautiful to be called his wife."

"So, he told you of his plans to marry?"

"Yes he has."

"Well that is a good thing. We are finally making progress," Sonya said grinning.

"I'm not so sure. I think Caesar is afraid of marriage and turning into an old hen-pecked man before his time."

"I don't think my husband will have to worry about that. He will need to stay spry and in shape just to keep up with me. I will keep him in shape and not let him get old before his time and I think I will start doing that tonight," Sonya said winking at me. "Come Caesar. I have some very interesting news to share. Good night Yellow Knife."

"What is my good friend Cooked Nose doing this evening?"

"When I left he was just sitting outside his lodge watching the people and enjoying the night air."

"Good then I shall go join him. I fear the air here will soon be too noisy to sleep."

Sonya laughed.

"Good night Yellow Knife. Tell my father I am with Caesar and I will not be home too late."

September 30th

I awoke to the soft sounds of rain pelting against the window pane and a smile across

my face. I don't know how many times Sonya asked me to take her last night but each time I

refused. She had come without her braves thinking the sheer passion of her lovemaking had

broken me but I explained that I was committed to Monica and until I had talked to her and

made her understand I still belonged to her. And Sonya used her every feminine wile to beak

me. There were several times during the night when she had all but broken me but she didn't

know and with the last thread of will I held on to my principles. That's not to say that

principles will stand up in the presence of a beautiful and charming woman. And like I said it

wasn't easy. But I did come to get to know the motivating force behind Sonya and I found

her to be both exhilarating and bright and during her long diatribe on everything from love

and marriage to the Cheyenne way of life I found myself several times wanting to grab her

and make sweet, passionate love to her. Yes, she had been right. She was a most attractive

woman but it was not that that aroused me but her stimulating conversation and passion for life that stirred the embers and kept my fire roaring. She was pulling me into the fold and no matter how much I was against the whole idea I was suddenly drawn to her.

I soon found myself riding to mamas. She was the last person I wanted to talk to if there was something on my mind. If she didn't look at me like I was a fool then her quick tongue would slice me up and toss me out with swiftness that would often times make me wonder why I went to her for advice in the first place. But by this time, I was so desperate that I went anyway.

"You asked me for my advice son so I'll tell you what I see from my perspective. I see a young man that I've raised and am so very proud of. You are a leader among men and you lead with promise, conviction and hope keeping the people's welfare first and foremost.

You are compassionate and caring. And because you are my son you couldn't help but be blessed with your mother's good looks. These looks help attract women to you and not just any women but beautifully attractive women. But because of your personality all that a woman has to do is treat you kindly. The problem you have my son is that you are a hopeless romantic. If they put the time in and treat with you respect then you are in love. The problem that I see is that you have yet to choose a woman. They choose you. And up until Sonya you weren't able to see it. Sonya was just the first woman that made no bones about her wants and desires. I like her because she is straightforward. Monica has done the same thing but she is much more refined in the undertaking. But ultimately it is you who has to make the choice. Man up and make the choice and stop letting it be made for you."

"So, what choice would you make mama?"

"I cannot pretend to know how you feel in your heart but I have lived and talked extensively with Sonya and aside from the alliance with the Cheyenne and just in terms of what I would want to see for my son I would say that Sonya is a better choice because of your values and the way that you were raised. Sonya has been raised to be a queen among her people. You have been groomed to be a king amongst yours. That and for no other reason do I see this as being a more favorable union. You share more of the same things, the same values."

"Thank you ma."

"I will discuss it with Crooked Nose later and see what he has to think."

"When is Monica due back?"

"The day after tomorrow."

"I do not envy you son but whatever you decide I will support you. Just remember that these are two wonderful souls so if nothing else be gentle,"

"I will ma," I said wondering if she would have come to the same decision if I'd told her of Sonya's visits.

October 1st

Monica rode in this morning and it was like Christmas. They said they were forced to buy three or four more wagons just to bring back the supplies and they could have sold off most of what they bought but my instructions were to bring enough back to stock Free Town's general store.

"We could have sold off the stuff we bought then turned around and picked up another wagon train full, doubled our profits and headed back here with a second wagon train but soldiers being soldiers were following your orders general. They make good soldiers but they aren't the smartest stars in the sky."

Seeing Monica was certainly a sight for sore eyes and it was certainly good to have her back in the fold and she seemed thrilled to be back.

"Any trouble?"

"Not really just the usual poor, red necked trash screaming obscenities but we ignored them and kept it moving. How have you been?"

"Not good but if you shower and change we can ride up to mamas and grab breakfast. Then we can talk about my troubles."

"Sounds good. I'm starved and tired of beef jerky and cold beans. Give me a half an hour then I'll come by and pick you up."

Riding home I thought about mama's words. 'You make the choice son.' and to my thinking the choice had been made a long time before Monica rode out.

I was awakened from my thoughts by a knock at the door. Monica walked in and I was shocked. Wearing brand new black leather boots and a coat I had never seen before Monica looked ravishing. Smiling she looked at me and said 'soon?' Opening the coat and letting it drift to the parlor floor there were no other words as I took her warm, naked body to the parlor settee where I laid her gently down.

"I need to talk to you," I said looking into the recesses of her hazel eyes.

"There will be plenty of time to talk Caesar but now is not the time."

How long I had waited. And Monica met my every desire.

Riding to mother's Monica chattered constantly.

"And yes if you're wondering I have given considerable thought to your proposal and have come to the conclusion that I do love you. But as far as marriage; I think it best that we

wait a year or two. By then we'll have established ourselves as business owners and ranchers and there will be less stress on us and our marriage."

"Hold those thoughts. It's all a bit much to take in right now," I said laughing and grateful that she had turned me down in lieu of things. "We'll talk Monica. Trust me we'll talk."

Mama's house always smelled good and today was no different as the smell of cinnamon and baked apples met us at the door.

"Smells good mama."

"Come on in. You're late."

Entering the kitchen I found papa and Aunt Petunia already seated.

"Monica darling it's so good to see you. When did you get back?"

"This morning ma'am."

"How was the trip," papa asked.

"Overall it was good. No real problems. At one time we ran into about a hundred or so Kiowa braves but once I told them of our affiliation with Crooked Nose there was no problem. All they wanted to know if we were with the Buffalo soldier leader that defeated Sheridan without firing a shot. When I told them I was engaged to him they escorted us to within five miles of the gates."

"So, you haven't told her yet?" mama said staring at me.

"No, mama I haven't had the chance."

"You haven't had the chance or the heart son?"

"Tell me what ma'am?" Monica asked nervously now. "That's all Caesar has been telling me since I got back is that we have to talk."

"Well, I will tell you since my son doesn't have the nerve. You should understand one thing before I start. Caesar is in love with you and has chosen you to be his wife and came to me for advice. I offered him no advice as he is a man and must make his own choices now."

Mama went on to recount the story of Sonya's marriage proposal. I looked at Monica as mama told her of Sonya's crusade. Monica dropped her head and I watched the tears roll down her face. When she was finished mama asked the now distraught young woman her feelings.

"What is there for me to say? The last thing I would want to cause Caesar is trouble and Uncle Ben always taught me that the good of the whole trumps the wants of the individual. I have never loved a man the way I love this man but he is bigger and means more to the overall welfare of the people than anyone else at Free Town so

I will sacrifice my love for the good of the whole. Do you mind if I am excused? Caesar please drive me home."

We rode home in silence. At times I'd turn to see how my girl was doing and though she never said a word to me I knew she was hurt. I admired her for having the strength and emotional resolve to accept the decision even though I still had not accepted it. I was still fighting to maintain my sovereignty although by this time I had all but given up.

"Monica I apologize. I should have been the one to tell you. Not mama. I tried to tell you when you first got here but you seemed so happy. I just couldn't bear to tell you."

"It's okay Caesar."

"No Monica. It's not okay. I have done everything possible to keep our people safe and out of harm's way and for some reason it's still not enough. Now they are asking me to marry a woman I don't love to strengthen the alliance that is already strong."

"It's a smart move Caesar."

"It may very well be but I shouldn't be forced to marry a woman I have no feelings for."

"That very well may be true but none of those people are in your shoes Caesar. They don't know the weight that you bear. They have no idea but it looks as though this is a cross you must bear for the rest of your life. Your life consists of no more than the community in which you serve. Funny thing is this may not be the worst of the demands placed on you. When Uncle Ben told me to watch over you I

never expected to fall in love with you but as much as I fought not to love you I still did." Monica said the tears flowing freely. "I expected the enemy to come from the outside. I never expected the enemy to come from within these walls."

"Well, it has. But now that we're together again we have to comprise a plan to stop this madness."

"There is nothing to do Caesar. The marriage to Sonya is the right thing to do for our people and the Cheyenne. You know that."

"But is it the right thing for Caesar. I would like a chance for some happiness in my life as well."

"I understand," Monica said. "But I think you gave the right to happiness

away when you accepted the position of being a leader of men. Tell me something

though. What did Fiona mean when she said she forced herself on you?"

It was truly agonizing telling her of Sonya's visits and her braves subduing

me but we had no secrets and if we were going to survive this latest challenge to our

happiness I had to tell her.

"No she didn't. Don't you see what that was about?"

"No but I am sure you're going to tell me," I said smiling and doing best to

bring some levity to an already grim situation.

"If it was just about the marriage strengthening the alliance between our

people then Crooked Nose's proposal asking you to entertain his daughter would

have been enough. If you had a mind to you could have weighed the situation and come back with an answer. But this woman is not thinking about an allegiance. She is a princess who has been given everything and for you to say you would consider it was an affront to her almost like who is this man to tell me no . Women have egos too you know. And this woman likes what she sees and will not be denied so if you even thought about denying her she has devised a way where you have no choice."

"Sorry. I'm not following you."

"I know you're not. You have to understand women Caesar. You may be a great soldier and general but of women you know nothing. Don't you see? She knows you and she knows that you wouldn't allow anything to come between you and her father's friendship so she's trying to get you to impregnate her. That way you wouldn't be able to say no to marriage. She knows that you are an honorable man and wouldn't do anything to defile her name by impregnating the great war

chief's daughter and then walk away. So, even if you should decide not to take

Crooked Nose's proposition to marry his daughter she is adding the needed insurance

to make sure you do."

I sat there dumbfounded.

"I'm telling you women are a treacherous sort. But then she could just madly

in love with you. And that I can understand," Monica said leaning over and placing

her head on my shoulder.

No sooner had she done this than a shot rang out causing the horses to rear

up. I pulled tight on the reins and grabbed Monica with my free hand to steady her

and stop her from falling.

"What was that?"

"I do believe that was a warning. She told me in no uncertain terms that if I didn't steer clear of you on your return some harm would befall you. Said if I truly loved you I would make sure no harm came to you. In other words, I am to have no contact with you."

"And you agreed with this?"

"Am I not here with you now my love? But I don't know if that's a wise thing in lieu of people taking pot shots at you."

"Okay Caesar. Let's look at it this way for the time being." Monica said visibly shaken. "You are the first man I have ever allowed to come to know me and I had no intention of doing that. When I left there was little doubt that I was going to be your wife. I just wasn't certain about the time frame. Now I am certain but in the meantime let's take a step back and reassess the situation. I will move so harm

doesn't befall either one of us.

I would appreciate you tending to my home and garden. I'm going to concentrate my time on expanding the library and Celeste has asked me to teach and supervise one of the schools. It should be open in a week or so. Between that and managing the general store in the evenings as well as managing and doing the books for the supply wagons I think my time will be pretty well occupied. This should give that little heifer all the time in the world to make you love her. And well I am comfortable with the fact that my man loves me I wouldn't suggest ol' girl getting too comfortable. She may very well be a princess but she has never seen a Black king or his queen threatened. She has never seen a woman hat will love and protect her man at any cost," Monica said smiling as we pulled up to her house.

"Keep going. I don't know when the next time I'll see you but I want this night to be one I will remember always."

I smiled and pushed the horses on. Arriving I noticed more than the usual one or two horses at Yellow Knife's ranch. I suspected trouble but knowing that my time was limited I grabbed Monica by the hand and led her in the house and up the stairs to the bedroom. Holding her in my arms I kissed her gently before undressing her and laying her across the bed. I don't know how many times we made love that morning but it wasn't enough. Each time I would reach an orgasm Monica would meet me screaming and letting the world know that she had reached another climax.

"One more time my love," Monica whispered in my ear. But no sooner than she said that than the bedroom door splintered exposing six or seven braves.

Reaching for my forty five on my dresser I felt the cold hard steel of a gun butt to the back of my head. It's hard to tell how long I was unconscious but when I awoke

there was Sonya surrounded by her braves sitting at my bedside holding a cold

compress to the place I'd been struck.

"I'm sorry Caesar but that wouldn't have had to happen if you had followed

my orders. I told you that she would not be harmed if you left her alone but no you

couldn't listen could you? "

My head was ringing.

"I don't know what you're not getting Sonya. This is the woman I love."

"This is the woman that you used to love. She has been replaced by a real

woman. Now she can sit and watch as I pleasure myself with her so-called man and

then she will swing by the neck until she is dead. And you have no one to blame but

yourself Caesar. Gag and bind the girl," Sonya shouted. "And tie him to the bed."

No sooner had they done this and placed Monica within arm's reach of the bed than Sonya stepped out of her clothes and began massaging Caesar slowly, gently Caesar turned his head away from Monica.

In only minutes Caesar was hard again.

"Why does your man respond to me if he is really your man?"

The tears rolled down Monica's face. Closing her eyes in pain there was nothing she could do to stop the woman's hurting words.

"You are about to die woman. Caesar could have easily stopped it if he had the ability to see what everyone else sees. We are destined to be together. It is inevitable and everyone has told him so but he does not tend to listen. Everyone cannot be wrong. It is you who are in the way. You have him distracted from our destiny. I am sure that you can see that our union is essential to our people's

progress. You can see that and yet you let your selfishness stand in the way. Well woman I have warned him and he still chooses you and now it is at your expense," she said grinding back and forth before laughing out loud.

"If it is this good and you are not feeling me my dear then I suspect we will have many sons my love."

When she had fully exhausted herself Sonya stood and took the gag from Caesar's mouth.

"I enjoy you Caesar although I am afraid I will have to sit in the warm springs tomorrow before I come back to see you," she said smiling as she bent over to kiss him. "Are there any parting words you would like to say to her before I have my braves do away with her?"

The tears gushed from Caesar's eyes.

"If you want me to ever see you as my wife you cannot kill this woman. If you ever want me to learn to love you cannot kill this woman."

"Then what do you suggest we do with her. She is a distraction that we do not need in our lives Caesar if we are to make this marriage work."

"Let me help her pack her things and then I will have her banished from Free Town once and for all."

"Do you see why she cannot be around if we are to make this marriage work?"

"I am beginning to. I will have her out of here by this time tomorrow. I will send word when this is done."

"I have your word that she will be gone by this tomorrow never to be seen or heard from again?"

"Yes, Sonya. Just do not harm her."

"For you my love I will show mercy. I will not send my braves. I will wait to hear from you. You have one last day to enjoy your play thing," Sonya said turning and walking out the door.

Sonya always loosened the bindings prior to leaving to allow Caesar to free himself. Today was no different. A half an hour later Caesar finally managed to get out of the rawhide stripping that bound him before untying Monica.

Caesar dropped his head in embarrassment.

"Don't you dare drop your head Caesar. You did more than any man could have done under the circumstances. And believe me it's apparent to everyone including her where your heart lies and that's why she feels that she needs to have me killed."

"What are we going to do?"

"We're not going to do anything. The woman was kind enough to give us twenty-four hours and promised not interrupt this time so I think after you run down to the creek and wash her sex off of you we can resume where we left off before being so rudely interrupted."

"I'm not sure I can do that now Monica."

"And I'm not quite sure I was asking you."

"And I'm not sure I can oblige. Lord knows I'm plumb tuckered out from all that sexin'" Caesar laughed.

"Yeah but now it's time for some lovin'. Now git Negro," Monica laughed.

Monica thought back. She'd been on the road for a month and the threats were real. Indians, soldiers and white settlers who wanted to shoot you just because and in this one day back she'd gone through more than in the entire month travelling through the badlands. Despite the day she was glad to have her man back even if it was only for a day.

When they had made love until there was no more Monica turned to Caesar.

"So, tomorrow I will be banished from Free Town?"

Caesar laughed as he reached over to the nightstand for his pipe. Lighting it he inhaled deeply before answering.

"Tomorrow I am taking you to the northern wall where Thomas the barber will cut your hair off. Boston will see that you receive a uniform. You will join his unit and I will have your own cottage build with all the trimmings and I will come see you once a day when I come to check on the troops. In the meantime I will take this woman in my home just long enough to get to know her weakness. And then…"

"And I believe we just found out one of her weaknesses."

"I thought you said that was merely a plot to get pregnant?"

"I thought so before watching her and listening to her moan. I think she enjoyed that just a bit too much. But go ahead you said that you would take her in your home find out her weaknesses and then... What's and then?"

"I'm not quite sure yet but in time it will come to me."

"And you know I'll see what I can come up with at the same time. Oh, and Caesar."

"Yes."

"I don't think you made love to me quite like you did Sonya. The way she was jumping around and moanin' I really think I got the short end of the stick."

Caesar laughed.

"You're not serious."

"Quite. But to put your mind at ease why don't you climb up here and try

again."

The two laughed and made love 'til the wee hours of the morning.

October 2nd

The day came in with a certain degree of sadness and though Monica wasn't

going far she was being separated from her man and another woman was moving in

with the expectations of winning her man over.

And because of her lineage and being a part of these elite Negroes who

believed in the individual waylaying their needs for the good of the whole she was

now expected to take the high road in lieu of everything.

What was taking place wasn't right. But what could she do about it? With all

her expertise and grooming when it came to trouble she was still at an impasse. She

watched as Caesar and Yellow Knife loaded her belongings onto the old buckboard

and before long they were off.

To make matters seem right just in case Sonya had some of her braves

watching Caesar made sure he drove Monica almost a half a mile beyond the front

gate where he gave her the reins to one of his finest young stallions. There they said

their final goodbyes before Monica drove her stirrups into the fine young animal and

they rode off at a gallop.

Caesar turned the wagon around slowly and drove slowly back to Free Town.

He noticed eyes watching from the side of the road and was aware that indeed Sonya

had had them watched. Summoning her braves he sent word back to Sonya as

promised. She could rest easy the girl was gone.

Passing his men Caesar relayed the message to Boston and Michael telling

them of Monica's forced exile and the danger she was in. Pleading with them to keep

a close watch on her and 'don't let her stray too far'. Caesar had to smile to himself when he said this. The last thing she'd said in parting was that she'd be keeping a close on him and she would never be too far away. And then she'd ridden away but not before looking back and saying 'soon'.

Oh, how he loved this woman.

Later that night under the guise of darkness she would sneak back in to Free Town. Here she would remain under the protection of my troops where she would remain until we have come to a viable solution and found a way to somehow solve the Sonya problem *if* there was a solution. When a rider came to tell me she was safe I closed my eyes only to be awakened by a knock at the door.

"Caesar. Please tell me it is true. My braves tell me you have put the girl out.

Tell me it is true."

"It's true Sonya. She's gone never to be heard from again."

"Now we can move forward. Kiss me my love."

Doing as he was told Caesar kissed the woman deeply, passionately.

"Will you take me and make love to me the way I know you can?" she said asking when only the night before she'd had me tied down and made my woman watch.

What kind of woman was this? Where was her heart? I did not consider any of this though when I made love to her. I was more intent on pleasing her gently, slowly. I wanted her to relinquish her everything to me and trust me while I devised a plan to rid myself of her once and for all.

In the days that followed I saw more and more of Sonya who seemed happy to show up at almost any time. One day she'd be there at the crack of dawn to fix me breakfast. The next she'd show up at mid-afternoon when she

knew I'd be working with the horses and join right in. To be honest she was a better horseman than anyone on the place and just as good a shot.

I would later find out that she rode with Crooked Nose's braves and had held her own in more than one battle. And still this did not endear her to me.

She was bright and loquacious and I enjoyed her company but remained a firm believer that one cannot learn to be in love. Love to me was spontaneous and once it has taken control of you it will often times feel like you're swimming upstream. There is nothing you can do but be consumed by it.

That's what Monica had done to me without once touching me or even attempting anything and yet I knew I was in love. I ate, drank and slept Monica. My every thought was Monica and when she left something inside of me died.

Sonya and I do not share those same feelings. At best we are friends although I am sure by her actions she is trying to quicken the pace and be more.

At night I make my rounds to check on my troops morale and just to say hello and for the most part they seem to be doing well. Many of them are working on their own private business ventures when not soldiering. I think if I had to name my most unhappy recruit it would have to be Monica. She is

grieving in much the same way Aunt Petunia did when she didn't know if Uncle Andrew was coming back or not.

I completely understand as she has been tossed out into the cold for no reason at all. I remember sitting on the front porch one night in late summer asking Monica why she had never taken on a beau and was surprised when she told me, 'I grew up in slavery and I watched and anytime someone became attached they were snatched from you she'd told me.

Slavery had taken her parents. She'd come home after being away years only to lose Uncle Ben. And then the first time she had the occasion to fall I love I'd been taken from her.

For the life of me I couldn't find a way to extricate myself from Sonya and when we met each night to see if any progress had been made I always felt like a failure.

Monica asked me questions about Sonya, about her habits and idiosyncrasies. I knew she was painting a picture in her head. She said at Oberlin where she attended the university they called it a case study but whatever they called it it was useless from her vantage point high above on this bluff far from town and even further from Sonya. That's what I thought until I caught the sun's

reflection off binoculars from someone high upon the hill that overlooks the corral.

I was careful not to give off my suspicions by glancing back but a soldier has a keen eye for what may be a foe lurking and waiting for the opportune time to attack. I had long since grown accustomed to Monica showing up unexpectedly but now was not the time. It was simply too dangerous and Sonya was finally begin to trust me and share more with me. Given a little more time she may very well give me something to work with.

I remember papa telling me how they had disposed of Missy Anne the slave master's widow who now ran Three Winds after slavery. They'd given her a lethal dose of laudanum which was untraceable. And I seriously considered this but it would have had to be administered while in her lodge and being that it was next to her father's it was well guarded. So, that was out.

At my wit's end I found my way to Yellow Knife's house to see if I could learn anything that would help me in my quest to eliminate my dilemma which seemed to grow in epic proportions every day.

"My friend I haven't seen you in—what has it been—two days now. Certainly didn't take you much time to grieve the loss of Monica," he said smiling.

At times like these I hated my friend but because I had my eyes on a larger prize I let the remark go. I was fishing now for a tid bit of anything that would lead the conversation to Sonya and he gave me more than I had bargained for when I asked.

"How do you keep your men's morale up when there are no battles to be waged?"

"I do not have to keep my men engaged. Between their families, your games and their raids on the Comanches they are not bored."

"Tell me they are not raiding the Comanches or anyone else. The reason we are in Mexico is to escape the killing and dying."

"My men are warriors. That is all they know. Many do not take to farming and raising cattle."

"But you were always the one championing peace when others wanted to go to war. Why do you now let your men attack the Comanche?"

"Because that is what the Cheyenne do. We have always fought the Comanche. I cannot explain it to you. Perhaps you need to ask your future wife why she is leading the raiding party tomorrow night."

This was news to me but I had to make sure that the information was correct. If nothing else it meant that I could spend the night with Monica. Later that evening when Sonya stopped by I angrily approached the subject of her leading the raid. She admitted that she was leading the raid but what Yellow Knife had failed to tell me that they were just taking coup and there would be no killing.

I refused to make love to her that night—well—at least I did until she hit me with the ultimatum.

"I will call off the raid if it displeases you. And I know that you are angry with me if you will not make love to me."

"Come to me." I said watching her face once again beam brightly.

Funny thing but this little turn of events did nothing for Monica who listened intently of the day's news but tonight there was no response. Monica seemed distant and aloof before informing me that she too had training and we would not be able to spend the night together as I had planned.

Between Monica and Sonya I was not only losing sleep I was losing my mind and there was no one I could talk to. Aside from Boston and Michael no one else seemed to understand my dilemma. And with no solution in sight Monica was becoming more distant while Sonya was doing her best to get pregnant or wear me out so I couldn't perform anywhere else. We could be taking an afternoon walk just talking and she would suddenly stop as if she'd forgotten something and say 'take me'. And as long as I did she was happy. She told me I was the first man she'd ever made love to and she loved it.

I couldn't tell.

The ranch was growing by leaps and bounds and I must admit Sonya jumped in and handled the books almost as well if not better than Monica. She was quick-witted and very bright with a charming personality and she was right. If Monica had been out of the picture or hadn't existed she may have had a chance but the fact was that despite her knowing it Monica did exist. I went to sleep and slept soundly that night.

October 3rd

There is a chill in the air today and as I look out my window I am surprised to find a steady stream of passerbyers many of whom are Cheyenne placing bouquets of flowers in and around the white picket fence which surrounds my yard. I'm somewhat confused and do not understand.

And there is a knock at the door and it is mother.

"I am so sorry son," she said. "For one so young to have so much sadness and sorrow in their life I am truly sorry," she said a tear running down the side of her face.

I still did not understand.

"What is it mother?"

"You really don't know do you? It seems your Sonya led a raid against the Comanches and was killed."

"What?! How did it happen?" I asked stunned by this latest bit of news.

"That's what Crooked Nose and his braves are trying to find out. I have just left him. It seems she was either hit by friendly fire or a sniper since she was leading the raid and was shot in the back of the head. But who would want to kill her? She was such a sweet girl."

She needed to say no more. I already knew.

Free Town

By

Autumn Sommers